THE OBERON ANTHOLOGY
OF CONTEMPORARY
NORWEGIAN PLAYS

THE OBERON ANTHOLOGY OF CONTEMPORARY NORWEGIAN PLAYS

Translated by Neil Howard

OBERON BOOKS
LONDON

WWW.OBERONBOOKS.COM

First published in 2019 by Oberon Books Ltd
521 Caledonian Road, London N7 9RH
Tel: +44 (0) 20 7607 3637 / Fax: +44 (0) 20 7607 3629
e-mail: info@oberonbooks.com
www.oberonbooks.com

This translation has been published with the financial support of NORLA.

PB ISBN: 9781786826978
E ISBN: 9781786826985

Cover design by James Illman

eBook conversion by Lapiz Digital Services, India.

10 9 8 7 6 5 4 3 2 1

Contents

Introduction
by Line Rosvoll

Writing from my experience here at *Dramatikkens hus* (The Norwegian Centre of New Playwriting), the fact that there is a growing interest in Norwegian drama across Europe is beyond question. The phone is always ringing and there are more and more artistic milieus across Europe that are specifically looking for new Norwegian drama. No doubt this is partially down to the spearhead of Norwegian playwrights that regularly get produced abroad. On the home front too, things are changing. Norwegian theatres are playing more new drama. Profiled novelists are shifting back and forth between novels and drama, creating a public interest for their dramatic writing too. There's a dedicated publishing house for Norwegian plays that's completely new and other publishers too are turning to plays. The public are picking them up to read and newspapers are even writing reviews! All in all, I experience a completely new hunger and interest for Norwegian theatre.

I guess readers of this book will wonder to what extent the works contained here are representative of contemporary Norwegian drama as a whole. To my mind, the very idea of 'representative' is almost impossible to consider. Here we have completely unique individual voices, completely unique types of projects. We have different types of dramaturgy and narrative structures, some leaning towards a more classical structure, others challenging the idea of genre or the idea of theatre itself – even a piece bordering comedy. I think playwrights in Norway are in some ways the true soloists; it is of course possible to work collectively and develop texts through working on the floor but, in the final analysis, they work with what's their own, often within a cocoon that they wrap around themselves. Retrospect is almost certainly needed for us to look back and fully understand what was actually going on. This is Norwegian drama now. If there is a common thread, it is not that these playwrights are determined to run in different directions from each other; it is that they want to express something that is deeply their own.

This sense of autonomy cannot be overemphasised. Two of the pieces here, Liv Heløe's *Why Not Before* and Eirik Fauske's *Grief Work*, take this one step further and are actually indicative of a rising trend in Norwegian theatre. In that both playwrights play the pieces themselves – are writing actors – they are, in some way, writing both *for themselves* and *to themselves*. And it's not simply because it's difficult to find work as an actor. You can see this phenomenon in the dance world too.

A while back I was working with a Czech director, Josef Krofta, and a Nordic group consisting of Icelanders, Danes and Norwegians. Krofta came up with a fascinating theory concerning the distinction between these three nations, which are often viewed as being very similar from outside. He asserted that Icelanders understand that the forces of nature are so much stronger than they are that they subordinate themselves to it and that this permeates the way they live their lives. The Danes, on the other hand, in their relatively flat country, feel superior to nature; they own it. Then there are the Norwegians, who are in an eternal struggle with nature. Is the mountain stronger or am I? Is nature going to win or am I? If the essence of drama is conflict, the crossing of wills, and the basic mindset is one of culture versus barbarisn or humans versus nature, then the Norwegians have a natural spring to tap into – and it is explosive.

It is evident that a nation's specific natural, historical and cultural heritage profoundly influences its drama and there is no doubt that there is a special core of 'Norwegianness' that you can see, feel, read and hear all the way from Henrik Ibsen and Tarjei Vesaas to Jon Fosse and Arne Lygre. Some elements, a direct relationship with one's own landscape, for example, are easy to trace: it is impossible, for instance, to think about Katrine Nedrejord's work without the background of her native mountains and the seemingly endless *vidda* of arctic Norway. Others are more elusive; what can be said is that a lot of contemporary Norwegian drama contains a sense of space.

Modern playwrights might Skype with one another or send each other texts but the space around them prevails; even here in Oslo, there is always space around us. The effects of this are at least twofold: Firstly, the space around us underscores a sense of loneliness, that we are alone in our battles in life. Secondly, this space makes itself felt linguistically, shaping style and form. Indeed, scholars, dramaturgs and professors around Europe often talk about the pared down language, the almost icy cleanliness and sparseness that floats above the heavier, psychological drama glimpsed below.

The influence of Ibsen is a strong element in itself that cannot be ignored. Not only do his works largely form the basis for how non-Norwegians view Norwegian drama as being serious, heavy and melancholic (which is actually by no means true about all of Ibsen's work), the very fact of his stature inevitably has far-reaching effects on Norwegian theatre as a whole. In fact, I can't remember a time when there wasn't an ongoing conversation about 'working in the shadow of Ibsen'. While on the one hand, he is undeniably a part of Norwegian writers' inheritance, he also limits the space that exists for new work. The institutional theatre continues to produce a large amount of classics, directors remain eager to bring their interpretation to the 'dead man's work', and actors long to create their own *Hedda* or *Peer Gynt*. At the same time, I don't think *Dramatikkens hus* would exist without him. In the wake of Ibsen, politicians cannot fail to be aware of the export possibilities of Norwegian drama, and have actively invested in and pursued that end for a good many years. One might say it is a case of both shadows and shoulders.

Here I would like to mention the ongoing wave of so-called 'Nordic Noir' as I think it quite possible that the almost universal enthralment with the genre may well have piqued further interest in Norwegian drama, despite its originating rather more in Sweden and Denmark. It is, moreover, primarily a genre that exists in film and TV. Theatre has to work in a different way. Violence here must be more in the shape of emotional violence, massacres of the brain, or the heart, or thought, not real physical violence or massacres because these can never be believable on stage.

Some, incidentally, believe Nordic Noir's fascination with social misfits and dark violence to be a reaction to the apparently peaceful A4 egalitarianism of Scandinavian social democracy. There may be some mileage in that view but, where Norwegian theatre is concerned, I think the reaction lies more in writers' wanting to break free from being pigeonholed or categorised. Many certainly don't want to be 'accused' of writing in a classical genre. In many senses, genres themselves are being put on trial. You might be reading a theatre piece and suddenly start thinking 'Isn't this a novel?' or 'Isn't this more of a poem?'.

Moving further into the social context, 'the world outside' often seems to think that, in respect of the country's affluence, high standard of living, national health service, stable representational democracy and relative equality, the Norwegians have 'got it sussed'. Indeed, when referring to Norway, foreign politicians such as Bernie Sanders, for example, during the last presidential campaign, and MPs from both sides of the house in the UK in relation to possible arrangements for a post-Brexit Britain, tend to hold up Norway as an example to be copied. Of course such views do not tell the entire story. While Norway regularly achieves the accolade of the 'World's best country to live in', we have surprisingly high suicide rates and there is an increase of young girls and boys seeking help with psychological problems. All the same, the relative lack of challenging exterior circumstances is perhaps why Norwegian playwrights keep returning to the more introspective themes of deep relationships – mother/father and family – and matters of the soul, heart and mind. In that sense, many modern writers are the true inheritors of Ibsen. While Kristofer Grønskag's *Kinder K* and Lene Therese Teigen's *Time Without Books* are not markedly introspective, and indeed draw on historical sources outside of Norway, if you look at the works in this volume, you'll find that they are all concerned, in one way or another, with the nature of human existence, exploring the ground through grief, loss, despair or a desperate search for identity. And this is no coincidence; of all the pieces that pass through *Dramatikkens hus*, around 90% fit into this description. Perhaps this goes some way towards explaining the success of some of our writers abroad: the deeply personal has greater universality than matters of greater outward scope. I remember Jon Fosse saying to me something like 'Make it so small that perhaps it will be big'.

The autonomy of writers and their exploration of the human condition through the examination of personal experience gives rise to what I believe to be a specifically Norwegian phenomenon, firstly in literature and now very much entering the theatre. This is writing as honestly as possible about oneself and one's own life: the literature (and now drama) of truth or reality, a kind of personal documentary, of which Karl Ove Knausgård's *My Struggle* is probably the prime example. Again we have a personal impulse reverberating outwards. Inside the theatre, I wonder if this new movement has anything to do with social democracy finding its feet within the old hierarchy. While the artistic director may still be king or queen of the hill, there are other requirements regarding artistic processes that are much more on the same level, that are very democratic. This is one of the ways in which independent theatre has been allowed to move in and challenge the institutions.

This 'democratisation' is also the result of the traditional divide between institutionalised and independent theatre now having been more or less washed away. The kind of theatre that was previously more independent has been drawn into the institutions with the result that the National Theatre has become absolutely one of our most experimental stages. Not only does this have a financial aspect, it is also the outcome of political will and a desire for cooperation. Artistic directors have been looking for ways to fill their houses, and stages such as the National Theatre have been the ones to open their doors to what might be called the avant-garde: wild groups that small theatres can't afford and can't take a risk on. Mainstream theatre needed to reinvent itself. To the extent that there still exists a divide between institutionalised and independent theatre, it is mainly a question of profile; you find the same directors, actors and material on all stages.

The washing away of boundaries also invites the blurring of strict forms. While prose is enjoying an ever-closer relationship with theatre (Heløe is now thinking in terms of theatrical essays, for example), young dancers seem to be increasingly concerned with language and words. Another dawning trend may be a return to more provocative, 'noisy', political material. *Ways of Seeing* (Pia Maria Roll/Marius von der Fehr/Sara Baban/Hanan Benammar) even hijacked the political agenda this year, which is amazing. People are kicking back a little more now, perhaps in response to the political shift to the right and the growing disparity between rich and poor. A kind of poesy is being maintained, but pieces appear to contain much more attack.

Finally, donning my director's hat for a moment, I would say that all the pieces in this anthology are pieces that I would want to put on. They're all disturbing and challenging and they all give me something to think deeply about as a director. And if you are a kind of detective, and wondering what Norwegians are and what Norwegian drama is – what contemporary Norwegian drama is right now – this will provide many of the answers.

Line Rosvoll
October 2019

Line Rosvoll is artistic director of *Dramatikkens hus* (The Norwegian Centre of New Playwriting), a national development and resource centre for new dramatic writing, collaborating widely with producers and communities within theatre institutions and independent companies, as well as fringe theatre environments. 'It's a kind of incubator, professional meeting place and "family farm" for playwrights to come home to.'

GRIEF WORK
Eirik Fauske

1. ARE THERE PEOPLE HERE?

i open my eyes
i'm sitting in a room similar to this one

outside the train window there are woods
power lines
a flat landscape

is this another country?
are we in another country?
aren't we in another country?
was that a field?
was that a road?
was that a house?

everything rushes past

was that a human?
is there a country here?
do people live here?
is it uninhabited?
what about birds?
are there birds here?
are there only birds here?
are there horses here?
aren't there horses here?
are there fish here?
are there fish in the rivers and lakes here?
and birds in the air and the woods?

do you live here?

do you live in a house or a cabin?
in a tent or a town?
huh?
are there houses and homes here?
is there town and country here?
are there mountains and snow here?
are there storms and wind here?
is there air and spirit here?
is there soul here?

are there souls here?
are there un-sold souls here?

everything flies, rushes, leaps, throws itself past

i move on
float on

floating air

is there a belief in soul and spirit here?

is there a lack of belief in soul and spirit here?
are there poets here?
are there lyricists here?
are there fiddle-players here?
are there
are there midwives here?

if there are midwives here:
are there births here?
aren't there births here?
are there caesarians here?
have they been invented?
have caesarians been invented here?

are there funeral directors here?
are there dead here?
are there dead mothers here?
are there dead sons here?

is there depression here?
is a darkness here?

is there a darkness in you?
is there a darkness inside you there?
hello?
hello?
everything is so strange
is there someone there?
is there nobody here?

am i all alone?

is there real joy here, and is this the centre of the world when
a child is born, are there blank sheets and music so unique
and sensitive that the hairs on people's arms stand on end?

is there an arm here?
was there an arm?
was there warmth here?

and

and is there joy here, if there's no joy here is there a darkness
in you a great darkness that won't go away that you barely
notice that you barely think about

so is it then light there's too little of or darkness there's too
much of, will a stream of light ever come in here, into life, to
the day, to the night

or is something completely new needed, a revolution,
something new to fight for, a new medicine, a new happening
a new falling in love a new start in a country in a town with or
without birds fish sea ocean sail out

or fruit on the fruit counter or arguing around the dinner table
or a hand in a hand

a hand a hand a little hand in your hand that slips into your
hand at night one night it's blowing outside and the darkness
has rubbed off on your children and i'm standing here in
front of this fucking rock wall, i can't get in i am all alone here
i can't
get

knock! knock! knock! knock! knock! knock! knock! knock!
knock! knock! knock! knock! knock! knock! knock! knock!
knock! knock! knock! knock! knock! knock! knock! knock!
knock! knock! knock! knock!
are you here?
where are you?

are there people here?

i see woods there are woods, an undulating landscape

5

i go on

after a while i saw a new hillside
crossed it, came to a marsh
crossed it, came to a bridge

is it Gjallarbru?
was that Åsemyrene that i just passed?
Grimaråsen, is that you?
hello?
is there anyone else here?

for i lay down on christmas eve
strength getting to sleep
strength getting to sleep

--

i go on

---

i get up
i wander on
i have to go now
i have to move on
i have to keep on going
come
come
come
come
let me go
let me go
don't turn round
don't turn round
i won't turn round
come

come

come

come

let's go

---

come

come

--

don't turn round

you mustn't turn round

2. THE SOUND OF THE SUN RISING

the sound of the sun rising

of small feet in the hallway

of bang you're dead

3. A GURGLING BELOW GROUND

across the plains, through the forest,
to the mountain, pounding, pounding,
through the mountain
through the mountain
through rock, stone,
to the other side
i'm standing in grassland
cattle, sheep, pigs round about
i hear water, but can't see it
rivers and streams below ground.
It gurgles. It calls.
It'll have to wait. It'll have to wait.
I want to go down but it'll have to wait. I can't give up.
I won't turn round. I must go on.

Cross a bog. Take out a tree with my axe. Whittle a stick.
Whittle a sword. Whittle a spade. The sun is upon me. In nine
minutes it will go down.

I trudge on.
Nothing for it but to go right on.
Nothing for it but to hold on.
Nothing for it but to hold out.
I have to get out of this. I have to get out of this.

I feel a breath on my neck. Is it your breath?

On the horizon i see the mountains of the underworld. High summits, peaks and mile-high waterfalls.

4. LOOK AT US

look at us
everything is chaos
the two boys have reorganised the living room
the sofa cushions are lying on the floor
i have to be a troll

and you are lying at the hospital, dead
i have just told them
i have told them everything
they understand nothing

and soon my sister'll come
and soon i'll take a cab to the hospital
stand in the room that was yours
hammer my fists on your chest
and lean into the wall

5. LARGE SINGLE WORDS

(impro)

NO
NO
ADSF
LJWØ
LFK-
JASD

ØFL-
KJASD
FREW
IT
GPRÅ
ASDF
LATO
FR
FOPRT
FRO
RASD
KFJ
PENG
AND
STILL
I
WENT
OVER
ALL
IS
OVER
ALL
IS
OVER
ALL
ALAL
ALAL
ALAL
ALÆA
SKLD
JGIO
ØAWR
OUT -
AWKJ
FÆPA
WOØD
SLFKM
EWLK
KPLEASE
PLEASE

PLEAS
EGODPLQ
ER
ASLKD
FJHELP!
LØAKS
DJF
ÆAØOL
SJFMA
JØALDKF
ASFAS
DJFALT
AØLKA
JSDF
ALL
IS
OVER
ALL
IS
OVER
ALL
IS
OVER
GAME
OVER
GAME
OVER
ALL
IS
OVER
ARØELKRAIN
ISSUN

CUDD
CUDDLES@
KAKSDJF
ØLLFKLØA
JSDNFKLKLVE
-KJAEG GJEKK VEGADKJM-AK.DJF A!!!!!!!!!!!!!!!!!!!!!!!!!!

6. AT THE HOSPITAL

up in the lift
along the corridor
people in green clothing
and at the end of the long corridor
a door
past a door
past another door
yet another door
and one more
then we sit
outside the room
that was yours

hands beating/pressing your chest
to lean into the wall
and then
look out of the window
a tree
in a wind
in rain falling

to a ground
to an earth

that is washed from under your feet

---

long enough ago this was ocean

7. THE LIGHT FROM THE TREETOPS

the light from the treetops
hit the grass
the forest floor
the print of a cranium in sand
seaweed over
mouth against glass in the evening light
family around the birch dining table

hands that held/clutching the tabletop tight
a storm, so silent
trees falling and a wooden ship
to let oneself fall
let oneself sink to the bottom
let oneself be found
(in a hundred years everything is forgotten)
by a diver with a torch or
a child's mouth or
a cranium against glass or
sunshine through the window half past five in the evening
the imprint of you eight years earlier in a sofa
the lighting hitting the glass, the water, blinding the skeleton
a storm in a wood and so silent
a storm in a wood in the water
we're foundering

we're foundering, you said
are we foundering, i asked
yes, we're sinking
and nothing can stop us
it's too awful
yes
it's unbelievable
it's unbelievable

8. FERRY

i'm standing on a jetty of planks
of logs of wood
i push out a boat

i go on board
i put money in a basket
i find myself a place
i sit by the side
i listen to the water

i feel the cold from the oar-strokes
i feel sleet on my face
and open my mouth
he sees me open my mouth
like a four-year-old on the way to pre-school

9. DIALOGUE VIDEO

are you there

i'm right behind you

are you there

yes

i need to look

no, don't turn round

i won't turn round

you mustn't turn round

i won't turn round

do you promise

yes
i promise
i won't turn round

10. THERE'S SOMEONE ELSE HERE

there's someone else here. Yesterday, in the woods, at the edge, in the mist, chopping a tree, i saw you, you were there, and then you weren't there, so i posted a message, which was returned, because there is no trace, there are no codes, there are no algorithms, there's only rumours, false, lying, hopeful, but not true, they can't be true, they can't be true, i'm standing in the supermarket, tears running in torrential streams, in rivers, in canyons, i'm unable to buy anything, where are you, where are you.

i have whittled these sticks, i have lit this torch, i have dug out caves in the mountain, i have swum to the deepest deep, i have climbed to the highest top, outside everything's small, crumbling, we are being eroded, i have been up in the clouds and down to the ocean bottom, all to look for you. look for you, look for you, all to look for you, look for you look for you, all to look for you, look for you, look for you

11. HUMAN HANDS

there is a cave here, with long shafts, passageways, blind alleys, large open empty spaces, huge halls, endless expanses of underground streams, rivers, oceans, stalactites dripping from the roof, abandoned mining tools, and there's one corner, by the way out, over there, where a strip of sunshine can be made out in the evening, the sunlight on the wall, and right there, when that happens, you can see the imprint of human hands, ten, twenty, maybe fifty prints of the same hand hundreds of times. i take the breathing tube, put it in line and blow powder over my hand, i have made a shadow. can you see me? i'm right here.

12. BEACH

a beach, early spring, cold, the ice has just melted, overcast, dark, wind, lots of sky, waves, debris. A family walks along with a little distance between them. walk beneath all the darkness, listen, see, lift shells, see a wooden ship, the woman holds the line of a kite. The man sits down, feels the grains of sand, they're cold, damp, the larger boy, maybe four, holds the other's hand, gripping it hard, in two months it'll be full of people here, today just these four, the boys find something at the water's edge, some object, run up with it, show it off, above are the clouds, strong wind.
look at this!

KINDER K
Kristofer Blindheim Grønskag

This translation was supported by the
Writers' Guild of Norway

For there is nothing heavier than compassion. Not even one's own pain weighs as heavy as the pain one feels with someone, for someone, a pain intensified by the imagination and prolonged by a hundred echoes.

– Milan Kundera, *The Unbearable Lightness of Being*

Characters
HE
SHE

The characters play a number of roles. This becomes clear in the text at the places concerned.

Although part of the action is set in a different time, the playing style, manner of speaking, costume and staging need not reflect this.

The facts concerning Gerhard Herbert Kretschmar's life keep to historically credible source material as far as possible. The dialogue and action, however, are wholly fictitious.

0

An apartment.

SHE is engaged in pottering about with a few of the small things in the apartment, does a bit of tidying and so on.

She takes a pot plant from a side table or window ledge.

She takes it into the kitchen.

Waters it.

Then she gets out a pair of scissors.

She snips off some of the dead leaves and stalks; makes it look a bit better.

She puts it down and considers it.

Straightens it up a little.

Considers it again.

Picks up the scissors again and starts systematically cutting off all the good shoots, all the flowers and flower-stalks until all that is left is a short little stump in the earth.

She puts it back in place.

1

There's a furnace some place where the fire never goes out.
Hidden, deep in the darkest woods you can imagine.
Almost invisible.
But it's there.
It is an insatiable fire.
An all-consuming sun.
Its thirst and hunger are all but unstoppable.
It gorges on fused fingers and hare-lips.
It delights in empty pupils and hearts lacking valves.
It gorges on the voices in heads.
A fire that warms us.
It has always been there.

2

HE
Look what I've found.

SHE
A picture of me.

HE
Nice.

SHE
No irony, OK?

HE
OK.

SHE
I can't be dealing with irony at the moment.

HE

I said alright. *(Pause.)* Horrible.

SHE

Thanks.

HE

You're welcome.

SHE

(Considers if the answer was ironic. Then refers to the picture.)
I'm drunk. I was too keen, drank too fast, got drunk.
Not drunker than everyone else. Just drunker faster.
Before the others in the picture. My dress is too short
and my cleavage's too low.

HE

You can see it: the boys think it's fun. The girls don't.

SHE

Half of them see me as a drunken opportunity.
The rest see me as… cheap.

HE

That's not very feminist, is it?

SHE

What?

HE

Everyone should be able to get drunk and dress
how they like. Their choice.

SHE

And…?

HE

Just not very feminist.

SHE

No. But true. *(Pause.)*

HE

But you do understand that picture isn't like what you are,
don't you? It was only there and then. It doesn't say anything
apart from what's on the surface. Nothing about what you're
thinking or what the others are thinking.

SHE

You can *see* what they're thinking… about me.

HE

That's just show. We can't ever know if it's real. Never.

SHE

You can see it.

HE

Where's the proof? We can never know if the body's
outside is a true picture of the body's inside. That's
old-fashioned. Almost racist.

SHE

Its inside?

HE

Your… soul, if you like.

SHE

A picture says more than a thousand words.

HE

No.

SHE

Doesn't it?

HE

No… Words can describe an inside from the inside's mouth.
Directly. Any single picture is dispossessed of any narrative.
It's only a moment. Never a story. *(Short pause.)*
One sentence can say more than any damned picture. *(Pause.)*

SHE

But you know the story.

HE

Do I?

SHE

You know what happened afterwards. It is – as they say – history. *(Refers to the picture.)* After this.

HE

Yes.

SHE

It was you who took it. Caught my attention. "Look! Someone's taking pictures," I thought. "What brilliant bloody fun." *(Pause.)* And after that…

HE

Yes?

SHE

(Smiles.) You took me home with you.

HE

Yes.

SHE

Who knows… Maybe that picture captures the precise moment I fell for you. And perhaps it should have stopped there. Hm? That the moment was interrupted. Deleted. Scratched out of reality. That nothing ever became of us. That I didn't go home with you. And into your bed. That I stayed behind instead. Got drunker. Threw up in the loo. Clambered into a taxi. Slept at home. And never saw you again.

HE

Maybe. *(Pause.)* This is the start of it all anyway.

3

HE, sitting in a waiting room with a baby bag. Nervous.

SHE

Gerhard Herbert Kretschmar. It's... that's what this
is about. Born in Pomssen, on the 20th February 1939.
It was a Monday. And we can pretty much assume for the
parents, Richard Kretschmar and Lina Kretschmar,
that it was a right fucking... blue... Monday.
One month after this Gerhard Herbert is born, it is 164 days
before a certain mister Adolf H. sends his *stukas* in over
Poland. And on this very day, one month after Gerhard's
birth, his father, Richard, takes him to his doctor in Leipzig.

(As the doctor.) Kretschmar, Richard. *(Pause. A little louder.)*
Kretschmar.

HE

(Nervous.) What? Yes. Here.

SHE

Please. Come in. So... what can I do for you?

HE

It's... Sorry, um... It's a bit embarrassing.

SHE

Alright... *(Short pause.)* Now. Listen. No need to worry.
We've seen pretty much what there is to see.
And... we will be able to find a solution for
your problem. That's why I'm here. To help you get
rid of your problem. So just breathe in. And then out.
And then tell me what's the matter.

HE

OK... *(Puts the baby bag down on the floor.)* There. *(Pause.
SHE gets up.)* But don't... Just... OK. Just look.

SHE

(Goes over to the bag. Bends down towards it and moves the quilt slightly to one side. At the same instant a sharp light shoots up from the bag. SHE leaps back.) Oh, for fuck's sake! Jesus!

HE

I did say...!

SHE

Fucking fuck! Can you...?! /

HE

/ You said..! /

SHE

/ Yes, but that was before I saw that! Jesus fucking Christ!

HE

But that's what it is. Whichever way you look at it.

SHE

But, fuck me...? No. Can't you cover it up?
(HE quickly pulls up the quilt and puts the bag a little further away from both of them. The light continues to escape from the bag but not quite as brightly as before perhaps.)
What...? I don't understand...
What do you want me to do with that?

HE

I...

SHE

I mean, fuck me, it hasn't got any feet.

HE

I know.

SHE

Only one arm. And if my suspicions are correct,
judging by its totally egg white pupils, then it's
blind as a fucking worm.

HE

I know…

SHE

We don't have any ointment we can rub on that, you know.
Which suddenly makes a new arm shoot out, or a couple
of new feet you can water every day. There's no eye drops
to scrape off the egg white, layer by layer, to reveal hidden
behind the smell of boiled eggs two baby blue pupils. There
aren't any pills for that! *(Pause.)* It's a…

HE

It's a monster. I know.

SHE

There's nothing I can do.

HE

(Pause. Whispers something to SHE.)

SHE

Sorry?

HE

Please.

SHE

No, I… /

HE

/ You said it yourself. There's nothing anyone can do.
No pills or ointments.

SHE

I'm not allowed to take life.

HE

But it isn't even a life. Look at it. Look!
(Pulls off the quilt again. The light shoots out.) A blind lump
of meat with epileptic cramps. You call that life?

SHE

(Pause.) I'm sorry… I can't.

28

HE

It's a stain. A smear against us, the family, the race.

SHE

I agree.

HE

So please just... /

SHE

/ No. I'll lose my licence.

HE

Please.

SHE

I said no.

HE

Well, I'm not doing it.

SHE

Nor should you.

HE

Not because I don't want to. Or can.
It's because it's a... an affair of state.
A matter of principle.
(Pause.) You won't help me?

SHE

I'm sorry, I... /

HE

/ Then we're done here. *(Picks up the baby bag and moves towards the door.)*

SHE

Wait. *(SHE gives him a pen.)* Write a letter.
Explain the situation. Ask for help.
I understand your situation. You have my
full sympathy, as they say. But I can't just...
I can sign the letter *with* you, OK? *(Pause.)* OK?

4

At the couple's house.

HE
(Stressed.) OK. So how long is it since last time?

SHE
How *long...*?

HE
Yes...?

SHE
It doesn't really matter how *long*, does it? The point is
I haven't got it.

HE
Are you sure?

SHE
Sure?

HE
Yes? Are you sure that you... just haven't... noticed it?

SHE
It's pretty difficult to miss.

HE
Yeah, well, what the fuck do I know... /

SHE
/ Yes, what do you know actually? *(Pause.)* Hm?

HE
You *asking*?

SHE
Yes, I'm asking.

HE
Well... it... um... It comes once a month. I know that.

SHE
And…?

HE
And there's… blood.

SHE
OK. Not technically correct, but I'll give you that. *(Pause.)*
And…?

HE
And what?

SHE
Anything else? *(HE searches for the words. SHE speaks
as if to a child.)* If it doesn't come, then… one is…
(both at the same time, overlapping) pregnant /

HE
/ Pregnant! I know that… I just thought there might be some
mistake. Or that you'd *counted* wrong or something.

SHE
Counted wrong?

HE
Can you please stop repeating every single thing
I say as a question?

SHE
I don't know, can I?

HE
You can see I'm panicking, can't you?!
I'm just not making any sense.

SHE
Are you going to panic like this when
the baby comes too?

HE
The baby?

SHE

That's quite often what you get, when you're pregnant.

HE

Fuck it…

SHE

You might well say so…

HE

Ohhh! Fuck it…

SHE

Aaaand you did…

HE

(Pause.) But the condoms?

SHE

What about them?

HE

You know what I mean.

SHE

OK… You remember when you came home from that party?
That stag do. You stood in the doorway, yeah, woke me up,
and stood there, stark naked with nothing but a tie around
your head. And then, you remember what you said…?
Comedian that you are. Hm? Remember shouting:
"I'm a rooster baby! Watch what my cock'll-do-to-you!"
Remember that, do you?

HE

(Laughs. To himself.) The rooster… yeah… *(Pause.)* Fuck.

SHE

You're so eloquent today.

HE

Just *once…*?

SHE
It's enough.

HE
Just ONCE?

SHE
Yes.

HE
Well, I'm obviously pretty fucking fertile then!

SHE
Congratulations.

HE
Thanks a fucking lot.

SHE
Can you stop swearing?

HE
Why?!

SHE
*(Holds her hands over her tummy, as if holding them
over the ears of a child.)*
I'd like "mummy" or "daddy" to be its first word.
Not "fuck". OK?

HE
Daddy…?

5

SHE is a child.

SHE
Daddy?

HE
Yes…?

33

SHE
Do you love me?

HE
Yes, of course I do. Masses.

SHE
Will you always love me?

HE
Of course.

SHE
Whatever?

HE
Whatever, my love.

SHE
Even if I do something wrong?

HE
(Slightly suspicious.) Like what?

SHE
Don't know. Just something.

HE
I'll always love you.

SHE
But what if… What if you wake up and I've been turned
into a monster?

HE
A *monster*?

SHE
Yes, one that frightens little children at night.

HE
OK?

SHE
Or that hunts people and eats them. Chews them up
in big gulps.

HE
Well, that's not very… /

SHE
/ Or what if I turned into a doll.

HE
A doll?

SHE
Yes, a little doll. Who can't talk. And that you have to look
after the whole time. Get me to sleep, eat, walk, dress me and
everything. Because I can't do anything myself.

HE
You and your imagination…

SHE
But what if that happens, Daddy? What then?

HE
Listen… I'll always love you. Full stop. OK? *(Pause.)* And now
it's about time my little monster went to sleep.

6

At Richard and Lina Kretschmar's home.
The light from the baby bag like a shard in the eye.

SHE
(Thinking. Then…) "Help to be put to sleep"?

HE
No. No, it must be more… more direct.

SHE
"Get rid of"?

HE

Then it can just be given away.

SHE

(Thinking.) "Removed"? No, that would be the same thing.

HE

(As if constructing the sentence as he says it.) "End a life which is not worthy of the name…"?

SHE

Yes… Yes. Say it again.

HE

End a life which is not worthy of the name.

SHE

Yes!

HE

Lebensunwertes Leben.

SHE

You're so eloquent.

HE

OK. That's it then… *(Clears his throat. Reads the letter.)*

Your people have a prayer. As good national socialists, we, Richard and Lina Kretschmar, have found it necessary to beg our Leader for help.

On the 20th February 1939, our child, Gerhard Herbert Kretschmar, entered the world. And although we so wished to see this child grow up to become a blond, straight-backed, blue-eyed hero in the ranks of the Wehrmacht, we must conclude that this can only remain a dream. The child was born deformed. It has no feet, only one arm and is, as far as we can tell, blind as well. We have, without success, presented our request to our doctor, namely to be relieved of this burden. Pursuant to the law not permitting such an action, our prayers have not been heard. But we cannot understand

36

how such a monster could be embraced by the words: One
people, one nation, one leader.

For this reason, we humbly beg our Leader's help. Help
us with this problem. *Lead* us. Help us *end a life which is not
worthy of the name.*

Your faithful servants,
Richard Kretschmar. Lina Kretschmar. And Dr. Werner Catel.

*(SHE runs to him and embraces him. A truly happy moment.
Suddenly, the baby cries. The light from the bag grows stronger.)*

SHE
It's hungry again.

HE
Feed it.

SHE
It's eating me up Richard.

HE
Feed it.

SHE
It gnaws my nipples with its empty gums. It's tearing them off.
Sucking out white milk and injecting mercury-grey poison.
I can feel it.

HE
It'll be over soon.

SHE
You've no idea what it's like. I'm disgusted every time it locks
its lips around me. I don't want it to touch me.

HE
I know… But it'll be alright in the end. *(Pause.)* Feed it now.

7

At the couple's home. HE in his own thoughts.

SHE
What's eating you?

HE
What's eating me…? *(Pause.)* That… test?

SHE
The amniocentesis?

HE
Yes. Why are we having it done?

SHE
Why?

HE
Yes. Why?

SHE
To check if anything's wrong.

HE
What do you mean *wrong*?

SHE
Haven't you read the brochure we were given?

HE
Yeah…

SHE
So you know then. There's all kinds of illnesses. Chromosome disorders.

HE
Chromosome disorders?

SHE
Yes. Patio syndrome, Edwards Syndrome, Fragile X…

HE

It's so unlikely that… /

SHE

/ But it happens.

HE

It happens… but there's a greater chance of killing the foetus
with the syringe tip during the test than there is of it having
any of that lot.

SHE

OK…? Well, that's good then. *(Pause.)* The sex.

HE

It doesn't make any difference if it's a boy or a girl, does it?

SHE

Maybe… I don't know. I'm taking the test and it's… /

HE

/ Why didn't you mention the last one?

SHE

What?

HE

The last one.

SHE

The last one?

HE

Yes? The last thing they look for?

SHE

What?

HE

(Short pause.) So that's why…

SHE

What?

HE

That's in the brochure too. *(Imitating her.)* "Haven't you read it?" *(Pause.)*

SHE

Down's syndrome, is that what you're trying… /

HE

/ It's not called Down's syndrome. It's called Down syndrome. Down! Not Down's. Everybody thinks that. But they're all wrong. There's no S.

SHE

Down syndrome?

HE

Is that what you're scared of?

SHE

(Short pause. As if there's a twitch in her tummy.) No. I'm not scared of it.

HE

What then?

SHE

I just want the best for my child. For it to grow up and be happy.

HE

It can… /

SHE

/ I don't know how many chances I'll get to have a child. Two? Three, maybe? Maybe ten, but I don't know, do I? I just want to use my chances as well as possible.

HE

In other words you're thinking about what's best for you?

SHE

What do you mean?

HE

You said you were thinking about what was best for the child.

SHE

Yes…?

HE

That's not what you're describing.

SHE

So what am I describing?

HE

(As if he wants to let the subject drop.) I don't know. Maybe it was nothing…

SHE

If there's something you want to say…

HE

No. It's just… nothing.

SHE

No… Nothing. *(Pause. Decides to pursue it.)* Do you know why you're coming out with all that?

HE

With all what?

SHE

All that shit you just said.

HE

Listen… I didn't mean anything… OK? We'll just… /

SHE

/ No, it isn't OK. I asked you something. Do you know why you're coming up with all that… that shit?

HE

No, but it sounds like you do…

SHE

Because you think a child with – Down! – syndrome will
increase your cultural capital.

HE

What?

SHE

Don't pretend to be all surprised. You can imagine it, can't
you? That everyone can see what a good person you are?
Hmm? A philanthropist. Someone who loves everyone no
matter what.

HE

My cultural capital?

SHE

You want to stay in fashion.

HE

In fashion? What the fuck…? You think that's how it is?

SHE

There's nothing more fucking modern and left-wing elitist and
you know it.

HE

So you ACTUALLY think that: that the only reason to choose
to keep a child with Down syndrome is to feel good about
yourself?

SHE

Isn't it?

HE

No.

SHE

Ask yourself. So you're telling me that it has *nothing*,
NOTHING, to do with how you want to appear.

HE

(Short pause.) No.

SHE

Why did you hesitate?

HE

So you're telling me it's wrong to do the right thing just because it gives you a good feeling?

SHE

I'm saying that YOU'RE in no position to call others egotistical, that's what I'm saying.

HE

Because it's left-wing elitist?

SHE

Yes.

HE

And modern?

SHE

It's like wearing a tweed jacket because you want to look clever. Exactly the same.

HE

(Short pause.) So this has nothing to do with you being a coward, then?

SHE

A coward?

HE

Yes... A coward.

SHE

(Pause.) Fuck that. Have you any idea how scared I am? Of ending up old and childless. Dry, shrivelled up. Unloved.

HE

All the more reason to... /

SHE

/ I want someone to look after *me* when I'm old. After me.
Not the other way round. You understand? *(Pause.)* Don't look
at me like that. You think you're better than me just because
you don't want to take this test? Is that what you think?

HE

No. I just want us to be honest about *why* we're taking the test.
Not to pretend.

SHE

Honesty? You want honesty?

HE

That would be great, thank you.

SHE

Alright… Call it maternal instinct if you like. Survival instinct.
Call it egotism if you have to, I don't give a fuck. The truth
is I don't want a sick child. It must be healthy. It must be my
healthy child.

HE

(Short pause.) Like all the others.

SHE

Yes.

HE

Normal.

SHE

Yes.

HE

Grow up in a healthy family.

SHE

Yes.

HE

And cut its hair like everyone else? Dress like everyone else?
Think like everyone else? Be a heterosexual, smiling child

with average grades, average height and a good income? Is
that what you want?

SHE

Yes. It is... /

HE

/ A completely normal average.

SHE

(Pause.) I just want to know if I have a healthy child. That's
all. *(Short pause.)* I've read about all the things that can
happen. The illnesses you can get. What can just turn up
while you're floating in there, weightless. All of them. With
pictures and everything. The internet's brilliant like that.
There's pictures of everything. And there was one picture
that really grabbed me. A new-born's hand. Of a child with
Edwards syndrome. *(To HE, sarcastic.)* If that's the right
pronunciation? Hm? *(Short pause.)* That picture... Something
happens to the hands because of the chromosome disorder.
The fingers get kind of... crooked. Bent over each other.
And this hand had the index finger and little finger bent up
over the middle finger and ring finger. *(SHE demonstrates
with her own hand. Becomes absorbed in her own fingers.)* And
there was something about it that awoke such an extreme
discomfort in me that I couldn't manage to look away.
I looked at those tiny, wrinkled fingers with their tiny nails.
Probably for several minutes. And then I noticed... the
discomfort... it had moved from my chest down into my
tummy. A kind terrible fear. *(Short pause.)*
*(Her two middle fingers have bent down towards the palm while the
other two point straight out... making the sign of the devil.)*

45

8

SHE

Reichsleiter Philipp Bouhler und dr. med. Karl Brandt, *die Kanzlei des Führers…* receive the letter concerning Gerhard Herbert Kretschmar precisely three days after it was posted. German efficiency, you know.

The case arouses interest. It illustrates a problem mister A.H. is already focusing on. As much as ten years previously, at the NSDAP conference, he presented a calculation as to how many mouths could be fed, houses built and young people educated, *just* by removing 70,000 disabled. A simple enough sum.

It is 140 days until England and France betray Poland. At the same time, the Kretschmar child is given a code name: Kinder K.

A few months later, on the orders of mister A.H., Dr. Karl Brandt finds himself on the train to Leipzig to examine the case more closely.

(Train noises. SHE enters the same compartment as HE.)

SHE
Oh, I'm sorry. *(Turns to leave.)*

HE
No, stay. Please. *(Gets up and does not sit again until SHE has sat down.)*

SHE
Sure?

HE
Absolutely.

SHE
Thank you. *(Sits down.)*

HE

(Silence. HE looks through the window. Breathes in.) It'll soon be
spring. Outside. Well… Inside too, but it's outside you see
it, isn't it? The crocuses opening. The bluebells ringing. *(HE
laughs gently.)*

SHE

Ringing?

HE

It feels like it. Ringing in a new time. *(Short pause.)* You
know… I've always thought spring to be the one season that is
closest to a feeling. One doesn't *feel* the summer. But one feels
the spring. Like a thrill throughout the body.

SHE

I… /

HE

/ Shhh. Just feel. *(Pause.)* Can you feel it? The spring? There's
a change in the air. A new time coming. Everything is to
change. The old has rotted under the snow and the fresh and
strong are to grow from the mulch. Can you feel it?

SHE

I can feel it.

HE

(Then, tenderly:)
Stunden der plage,
Leider, sie scheiden
Treue von Leiden,
Liebe von Lust;
Bessere Tage
Sammlen uns wieder,
Heitere Lieder
Stärken die Brust.

(HE expectant. SHE thoughtful.)

47

SHE

Goethe..?

HE

(Smiles broadly.) Very good… *(Pause.)*

SHE

(Looks out.) Where are you going? Dresden?

HE

Leipzig.

SHE

Holiday?

HE

Work.

SHE

Really? What do you do?

HE

(Smiles. Pause.) Have you read the Jewish stories?

SHE

(Shocked.) Why on earth… /

HE

/ Know your parasite, that's my motto. *(Laughs. Short pause.)*
Do you know what a golem is?

SHE

No.

HE

The Jews' monster. Made of clay. From earth we've come and
so on and so forth… An unformed creature, without human
features. Like, but not like. Unthinking, violent and repulsive.
Created for the Jews' protection.

The most famous story concerns the Prague rabbi, Judah
Loew ben Bezalel, who created one of these golem because
he was tired of the poor treatment the Jews were receiving.

You know, pogroms and all that. He shaped it from the mud
of the Vltava riverbanks. An enormous, lifeless, mud-man
in the synagogue. And he whispered into its ear: "Protect
us. Find our enemies' children and tear them in two.
Find our enemies' wives and drown them in the river.
Find our enemies and erase them from the face of the earth.
Protect your people."
And so he gave it life… *(Short pause.)* You know how to bring
a golem to life? *(SHE shakes her head. HE bends down closer.)*
One takes a knife to the soft mud of the forehead…
(HE writes on her forehead with his finger.) … and incises the
word 'emet' into it.

SHE
'Emet'…?

HE
Hebrew for 'truth'.

SHE
'Emet'.

HE
Truth. And then… After the golem has carried out the Jews'
commands, when it's no longer useful and only a burden, an
uncontrollable, dangerous alien, what does one do then?

SHE
What…?

HE
One has to take its life.

SHE
How…?

HE
It's simple. One takes the same knife… *(demonstrates with a
finger as previously)* and one cuts away, scrapes, scratches and
rubs until the first letter in its forehead is no longer visible:
The letter 'e'. So it now reads…?

49

SHE

'Met'…

HE

Death. *(Short pause.)* To earth you shall return…

SHE

'Met'.

HE

The power of a word. Isn't it incredible? Simply by removing one little letter. From truth to death.

SHE

So what exactly is it that you do…?

HE

My job is to *carry out* the power of the word. *(Pause. Smiles. Declaims.)* I am the word. In the beginning was the word, and the word was God.

9

A bar.

HE

You should be getting off now.

SHE

Hm?

HE

We're closing. Sorry.

SHE

Closing…? You can't just close up like that.

HE

Why not?

SHE

We're celebrating. You can't close when we're celebrating,
now can you? *(Short pause.)* Well that's the end of the party
then…

HE

(Looks at her. Pause.) Five minutes.

SHE

Five minutes! That's the fellah! Five minutes… Hah! Think
how much can happen in five minutes. Even if it's a… an
infinitesimal amount of time really. Almost nothing.

HE

The blink of an eye.

SHE

Too right to deny! *(A little surprised.)* Hah! That rhymes.

HE

(Pause.) What's the occasion?

SHE

What?

HE

You said you were celebrating…?

SHE

Did I…?

HE

You did.

SHE

Yes, I suppose I must have. *(Short pause.)* The greatest miracle
of nature. The creation of life. The propagation of the species.
Generation upon generation and so on. *That*'s what we're
celebrating.

HE

Right…?

SHE

Yep. I'm pregnant, aren't I?

HE

(HE takes her wine glass.) You shouldn't be… /

SHE

/ *(Uses one hand to hold HE away; uses the other to empty her glass. Then, provocatively:)* Ahhh! There you are. *(Gives HE the empty wineglass.)*

HE

You know you're not supposed to… /

SHE

/ Ah! It can't get any worse.

HE

(Pause.) Perhaps you should go now?

SHE

Perhaps I *shouldn't* go now?

HE

Can't you just… /

SHE

/ I've got two minutes left. You said five minutes and I've only had three. I've got two left. And you know what I'm going to do in those two minutes?

HE

No?

SHE

I'm going to tell you a story.

HE

OK?

SHE

OK. Ready? Here it comes. *(Short pause.)* Imagine that I'm eight years old. A little girl. Can you see it?

HE

Yes.

SHE

Good. And now imagine it's Christmas morning. Your
actual Christmas morning. And I jump out of bed... That's
something people say; you don't really jump very much.
It just means you get out a bit quick. Understand?
Eager, you know... /

HE

/ I understand.

SHE

Good. So I hop out of bed, run down the stairs in my
pyjamas and see the Christmas tree. The whole house has
been decorated overnight. By Father Christmas, obviously.
There's gold everywhere, glitter, baubles. There's a fire in
the fireplace, it's lovely and warm and smells safe. Under
the tree there's a great big pile of presents in all shapes and
sizes. And they're nearly all for me – you know, only child.
(Short pause.) And then... then I see one parcel that stands out
from the rest. It's a bit on its own, a little bit apart from all the
others, but most important of all it's got a huge ribbon on it.
An enormous red silk ribbon. A bit kind of Disney up to now,
don't you think?

HE

Absolutely.

SHE

But childhood was a bit Disney-like, wasn't it? If you try and
remember?

HE

It was.

SHE

And it gets better. *(Short pause.)* Before it gets worse.
Because... I go over to the present. And I see that it's got

small holes in it…? And then I realise… Of course, they're
air-holes.

Like for a little puppy. *(Smiles.)* And I've always wanted a
little puppy, as long as I can remember, and I'm so happy. So
I reach up, get hold of the ribbon and pull. It comes undone
completely perfectly. Like a piece of choreography. And I
take the lid and lift it off. And there…! There's a little puppy
lying there. Brown, with white patches on its raggedy ears. It's
the most beautiful puppy in the world and I get tears in my
eyes just looking at it. So… I carefully put my hands around
the puppy and lift it up and give it a kiss. *(Short pause.)* And
it's *then* that I notice it.

HE
What?

SHE
That it's all limp. Kind of heavy, if you know what I mean.
Or empty perhaps. It's not moving. Not breathing. So I shake
it a bit. Try to open its eyes with my little fingers. But it's no
good. *(Short pause.)* And then my dad comes in. He's been
watching and has understood what's happened, so he comes
running in and tries to take the puppy off me. But it's *mine.*
(Demonstrates unconsciously with her hand.) So I hold it tight.
I remember the sound, and the feeling of the tiny little puppy
bones giving way to my thin little fingers. Tiny little crunches.
And Dad tries to force my hand open, but it's my puppy, isn't
it, it was exactly what I wanted, my present, and I just squeeze
it tighter and tighter. *(To HE.)* End of Disney.

HE
Jesus…

SHE
When Dad finally manages to get my fingers open, the puppy
is completely… broken. Its guts are poking out from a little
wound on the side. Its eyes have burst. And I'm standing
there with all the goo on my fingers. *(Short pause. Thoughtful.)* I

don't think he ever buried it in the garden… *(To HE.)* End of
story. Running over a bit but… *(Short pause.)*

HE
Is that true?

SHE
It's never quite like what you imagine, is it? *(Short pause.)* Just
like what you fear. Do you understand what I'm trying to say?
What the story's really about?

HE
(Pause.) Maybe it's time for you to go home now?

10

SHE makes splashing sounds in some water.
HE is a child being bathed by its mother.

SHE
Time for a little bath? *(SHE splashes in the water.)* Is it warm
enough?

HE
Yes.

SHE
There we are… now you'll be all nice and clean. Just a little
bit of soap in your hair.

HE
Nooo.

SHE
I'm afraid so.

HE
But I get it in my eyes.

SHE
Not if you look up at the ceiling. That's it. Up here.

HE

I'm looking.

SHE

That's it. And now rinse…

HE

(Splashing.) Oooohhh…!

SHE

There.

HE

(Pause. HE hums a little bit of an undistinguishable song.) Shall
I hold my breath? Time me. Under water. Ready? One…
Two… *(HE takes a deep breath. SHE splashes in the water. Pause.
Then HE gasps a new breath.)*

SHE

Twelve seconds.

HE

I wasn't quite ready. Again. One… Two…
(HE takes a deep breath.)

SHE

*(Splashes in the water with increasing intensity. SHE breathes a
little heavier. He makes small sounds, as if he is under the water
a little bit too long. The splashing becomes less, and intermittent.
Silence. The silence is broken by HE gasping for air.)*

11

*At Richard and Lina Kretschmar's home.
They are not there, but doctors Karl Brandt and Werner Catel are.*

SHE

(Light escapes from the baby bag, illuminating the scene. Gasps.)
You try and pretend it's a perfectly normal sight, but it simply
isn't, no matter how often you look at it.

HE

Dr. Catel, 'normal' has nothing to do with *quantity*.

SHE

No…

HE

So this is Kinder K, in person, no less? *(Short pause.)*
Fascinating…

SHE

What is?

HE

That nature can produce something so unnatural. Don't you
think so?

SHE

I guess…

HE

But then on the other hand… weeds are also a kind of
flowers, aren't they?

SHE

Flowers?

HE

And the bed has to be weeded regularly. Keep them from
strangling the roses. That would be a shame.

SHE

Yes, it would.

HE

(To the child.) Little golem, I think you and I are going to
become good friends.

SHE

(Short pause.) It erm… It's lacking a number of limbs, as
you can see. And it's a bit early to say but I suspect that it's
blind too. And it sometimes enters a kind of epileptic state…
Violent convulsions. Of course, it's only my opinion but…

HE

Idiot?

SHE

Sorry…?

HE

An idiot? Is he an idiot?

SHE

Yes. Most probably.

HE

It's perfect. This child… it's going to outlive us both. Despite its imminent death. Its name will herald the start of a new era. A cleaner, more humane future. *(Short pause.)* There'll be books written about it. It's going to live forever. Become a symbol rather than a human being. Not born for life, but born for eternity. And right now, it's just lying there, floating somewhere in-between. You've met the parents, of course?

SHE

Yes.

HE

And how would you characterise them?

SHE

As afraid.

HE

Afraid?

SHE

Full of fear.

HE

Of what?

SHE

Of that. Poor people, they're absolutely desperate… You know, they came to me. Asked me to take its life. That's the last resort. The last cry for help.

HE
(Sincerely.) Poor people…

SHE
They've had to bear more than their fair share.

HE
And now it's high time we bear ours.

SHE
Oh?

HE
Social hygiene is about to make its entrance. *(To the child.)*
Young Master Kretschmar here will be the first. But not the
last.

12

At the couple's home.
They're lying next to each other. Intimate.

HE
You're the last person I'd wish anything ill… I'm sorry.

SHE
What for?

HE
It wasn't supposed to be like this. Sorry. *(SHE does not
respond.)* Do you know what was the first thing about you
that I fell in love with? *(Short pause.)* Your little heart. You
probably think it's stupid but… *(SHE doesn't understand.)*
When you had fallen asleep. After the picture. That first
night. Your breathing was so… short. Short and quick. And
I thought breathing like that could only possibly belong to
a little heart. Like a bird's heart, or a child's heart. And I
suddenly wanted
to just look after that little heart. Put my hand around it and

feel the tiny heartbeats in my palm. *(HE squeezes her hand. They smile a little.)* I will look after it now as well. *(Pause.)*

SHE
I can't see how this is going to work.

HE
It'll be alright.

SHE
How?

HE
We'll be doing it together. So it's bound to be alright.

SHE
Is it?

HE
Yes.

SHE
You think my heart can bear it?

HE
I'll carry it for you, if you ask.

SHE
We'll try again.

HE
Of course.

SHE
And then everything'll be different, won't it?

HE
For sure.

SHE
(Short pause.) It feels like it's my fault /

HE
/It isn't.

SHE

Like I'm *already* a bad mother or something /

HE

/Don't.

SHE

Before I've even become one. Beforehand.

HE

You mustn't think like that.

SHE

So how am I supposed to think?

HE

Think that there's room enough in my hands for another heart. Remember that. You're going to be a great mum.

SHE

Another heart? What are you talking about? *(SHE pulls her hand away.)* Haven't you understood?

HE

What?

SHE

I'm not going to have the child. There... I've said it.

HE

But we... /

SHE

/ No... No. You must listen to me. Listen.

HE

I'm trying to... /

SHE

/ You listen to my heart...? You can listen to that alright. But not my voice.

HE

It doesn't always make sense.

SHE

Neither does my heart. It just fucking doesn't.

HE

I *hear* what you're saying…

SHE

So understand it then… I don't want to. You understand those four words? It's that simple. *(Short pause.)* I don't want to.

HE

You don't want to?

SHE

No.

HE

Why not?

13

Light up from the baby bag. Dr. Brandt and Lina Kretschmar.

SHE

Why do you ask?

HE

Forgive me, Mrs. Kretschmar, but… Call it curiosity. Understanding.

SHE

Because that's the way it is. You've seen it yourself now.

HE

But it could just have… been. Couldn't it? Existed? There isn't any real need to… yeah.

SHE

But that's what I want.

HE

Because it's weakness embodied?

SHE

No. *(Short pause.)* Maybe it's like that for Richard.

HE

Oh?

SHE

He hasn't managed to get an erection since it was born.
I've tried but... I can see he's thinking about it. When I go
down on my knees and... or if I just kiss him. Even if he
closes his eyes, I can feel that he's thinking about it. Just goes
completely limp. There's not even a little man left in there.

HE

What about you?

SHE

Me? I just think it's best for everyone.

HE

For it too?

SHE

Yes. *(Short pause.)* Compassion. You know what that word
means? Really? To suffer with someone. My pain on its own
is nothing. Well... not nothing. It's dreadful. But... I can cope
with that; you just do. But mine, his and its pain... all at the
same
time. *(Refers to the child. Shakes her head.)* There's too much
suffering collected in that little deformed body. So that's my
'why'... Compassion.

HE

The best for everyone?

SHE

That too.

HE

More than you know.

(Whispers.) Action T4. *Tiergartenstrasse 4.* Head office of the *Gemeinnützige Stiftung für Heil- und Anstaltspflege.* An address which will become synonymous with compassion.

On the 1st September later this year, I'm going to receive a letter from our leader, where it says: "*Reicshleiter* Bouhler und dr. Karl Brandt are hereby given the task of increasing competence among individual doctors so that patients who are considered incurable, on the basis of human judgment may be permitted a merciful death after thorough medical evaluation".

This is the work we are to begin. By the end of 1941, with our increased competence, we will officially have given the gift of a merciful death to 70,273 people. And it will continue. The figure will end up around 250,000. But this is just a small part of the whole. Just the beginning of something even bigger. We are going to eradicate all illness, all weaknesses of the flesh and mind forever. The greatest humanist project anyone's ever seen. It will astound the entire world. *(Pause.)* And Gerhard... will be the first.

SHE

How will we be remembered?

HE

As brave.

SHE

Is that what we are? *(HE nods.)* Will it hurt?

HE

One forgets so quickly.

SHE

No. Not me... It?

HE

(Short pause.) Do you think it understands pain?

SHE

Even an animal understands pain.

HE

It won't notice anything.

SHE

So how…?

HE

We'll provide an overdose of the medicinal drug, Luminal.
It'll just go to sleep.

SHE

And not wake up…

HE

A time will come when we'll need to be more efficient, but it
hasn't come yet. This is just an individual case.

14

*Night. A faint light emanating from the baby bag, as if the light is
asleep. HE undresses. Comes in naked from the bedroom.
Sits down beside the baby bag. Talks to the child.*

HE

You are mine…

Despite everything… you're mine.

And I'm yours. Completely in your power. You have recreated
me. Transformed me into something that I wasn't before.

When you were born, I was reborn. Redefined.

We were ordinary people before, but now you define
everything. Nothing exists outside of you. Not me. Not her.

We are imprisoned in you. We *are* you. And I can't cope with it being like this.

I keep telling myself that I'm doing you a favour.

Because you *are* what would have eaten you too one day. You are the first hospital with high walls and locked gates. With buses shuttling back and forth. Where all go in and none come out. The first signature. The first canister of gas. Hidden vents beneath the benches. You are randomly mixed ash in an urn. You are the first. And you are mine.

They're going to say it was done by force but the statistics will show that that certainly wasn't always the case. They won't mention that.

They'll build museums to remember but they'll forget like always. They won't mention that either.

So I tell myself again, I'm doing you a favour.

Because there's no place for you in this world just now. It's a world of cold steel that is emerging. One where we can't bear to see that we are one cell, one chromosome, one scissor snip away from perfect. You wouldn't have survived a world of steel.

And maybe that's true?

(Pause.)

Or perhaps it's that I'm repulsed by the sight of you. That it's unfair that I got you. That I can't manage to fuck my own wife. That the world deserves to burn.

(Short pause.)

Or maybe it's all these things at once? Perhaps it's all true?

15

SHE comes into the flat, wearing an outside jacket.

SHE

Hallo…? Where are you? *(No answer. A little louder.)* Hallo?

66

HE
(HE dries his hands on a rag.) Hi… I've been trying to get hold
of you.

SHE
I know…

HE
Where've you been?

SHE
Just at a friend's house. Relaxed.

HE
OK… Everything alright?

SHE
Yeah, it…

HE
I've made some food. Want some? *(SHE nods.)*
Just something simple.

SHE
That's nice.

HE
OK…I'm glad you're here.

SHE
Me too.

HE
Shall I help you with your things? *(Helps her get her jacket off.)*

SHE
Thanks.

HE
(Looks at the jacket.) Agh, shit…

SHE
What?

HE

Sorry, I… I think I got a bit of paint on it… Bollocks.

SHE

Paint?

HE

Yeah, I… *(HE looks at her. Puts down the jacket Then…)*
Come. *(Takes her hand.)* Are you ready?

SHE

For what?

HE

Are you ready?

SHE

I don't know.

HE

Can't you just say 'yes'? *(SHE shakes her head. HE opens the
door to a green-painted child's bedroom.)*

SHE

The office…?

HE

I chose green. So it wouldn't be either blue or pink. It's a bit
old-fashioned. *(Pause.)* Do you like it?

SHE

These are all my things.

HE

Yes, I… /

SHE

/ This is my mobile… I can remember it… over my cot…

HE

I went over to your mum's. Went and got some of your
old things.

SHE
You did?

HE
Isn't it nice? All your old things…

SHE
Jesus…

HE
What?

SHE
Who are you?

HE
What?

SHE
What are you?

HE
I thought… /

SHE
/ What the hell is this supposed to mean? What's the point?!

HE
It's just a room.

SHE
A room? These things are all fucking mine. *(Tears down some of the things HE has hung up.)* Mine. Not some other kid's.

HE
It was well meant.

SHE
Well meant?

HE
Yes.

SHE

(Starts hitting him.) Well meant? Well? How can you say that?
That it was WELL MEANT? /

HE

/Don't! Hey! Stop it! *(HE grabs her and throws her down on the
ground. Silence. He goes over to help her up.)*

SHE

Don't! *(Does not let HE help her.)*
Finally. Finally you're doing something honest.

HE

I'm sorry, I… /

SHE

/ DON'T say sorry.

HE

I didn't mean to.

SHE

Yes, you did.

HE

No.

SHE

Yes! And have you any idea how good that is? Have you?
Finally seeing you do something spontaneous?

HE

Spontaneous?

SHE

Something which hasn't been considered to death? /

HE

/I was angry. I shouldn't have…

SHE

To actually see you do something selfish. Do you know that?
(Gets up. Pause.) You know what… that actually gets me a bit
excited. *(Groans.)*

HE

For fuck's sake… /

SHE

/ Do you want to feel how wet I am? Come on. Feel.

HE

Can you… /

SHE

/ No? Not even a little bit? Just a couple of fingers?

HE

No!

SHE

Cause you know I like it rough. Of course the problem is
just…. That you're not rough *enough.* Isn't that right?
(SHE slams her body against the floor.)

HE

Stop!

SHE

If you're going to do it, you might as well do it properly!
(Throws herself again.)

HE

(HE grabs her and holds her tight.) That's enough!

SHE

What are you going to do? Hold me? Tie me down? For how
long? You'll have to let go sooner or later. At one point or
another you're not going to be there to look after me. And
who knows what I'm going to do then? Perhaps I'll throw
myself down the stairs? Drink turps? Pay someone to give me
a good hard kick in the belly? And you won't be there to
stop me.

HE

(HE lets her go. Grabs the mobile and breaks it. Silence.)
What do you want from me?

SHE

Understanding.

HE

But it's incomprehensible to me.

SHE

(Referring to the child's bedroom.) So you do all this to…what?
Convince me?

HE

I don't know. I just…

SHE

You just what…?

HE

What if this room wasn't empty. Imagine how brilliant
that would be. All the happy memories that would be
created here.

SHE

With all my things?

HE

Yes.

SHE

What were you thinking?

HE

Don't know… I… *(Pause.)* Where do you think imagination
comes from?

SHE

What?

HE

In the body? Because that's what makes it hurt. *(SHE doesn't
reply.)* I used to think it was in the brain. Before. Not anymore.
It's further down. In the upper body somewhere. It hurts like
fuck. I hate it.

SHE

What do you mean?

HE

Are you not listening? It never stops. Constantly whispering
in my ears. Asking questions. *What would your life be like if
you'd chosen that girl? What if it was her you lived with and loved,
and she loved you? What if you'd dared make that choice? Or what
if you'd had another job? Different education? Are you living in the
right town? There's so much out there to see in the world. Imagine
what the child might be like. What everything might be like.* And
so it goes on. Stops when I sleep but starts again the moment
I wake up. Like an echo from the day before. And the day
before that.

SHE

(Pause.) I know what you imagine.

HE

Do you?

SHE

You imagine all the good things. The sunshine stories. The
wonderful moments. And of course there would be some
of those, but… *(Short pause.)* In all those moments your
imagination whispers in your ear… Does it rain in any of
them? *(HE doesn't answer. SHE gives a brief laugh.)* That's
what I thought. That's what you think about, isn't it? The
good things. Not about the thousands who have to live in
institutions. In old people's homes. So you can say you live in
a diverse society. We sacrifice them willingly. But is that what
they want? Do they have a voice that gets heard? And who
speaks their language?

HE

You maybe…? *(Shakes his head. Pause.)* Can you hear yourself?
I don't understand the kind of mouth that's coming out of.

SHE

I'm just saying that not everything's black or white.

73

HE

No, you're saying everything's black.

SHE

I'm saying what I feel. And you're saying that that's wrong.

HE

I'm saying that it's cowardice.

SHE

You're blind.

HE

You're trying to foist the decision on someone else.
Or something else, outside of yourself. But it isn't. You think
it's a collective decision. But it's only yours.

SHE

Yes *(Short pause.)* Only mine.

16

Light form the baby bag. HE is Dr. Brandt.

SHE

It is the 25th July, 1939. A Tuesday. Thirty-eight days before the
invasion of Poland. Gerhard Herbert Kretschmar, who, until
2007 was known only as Kinder K, is 156 days old. It is now.

Dr. Karl Brandt fills his first syringe with the epilepsy
medicine, Luminal. He is to lead the euthanasia programme,
the programme for mercy killing. He will later face judgment
at the 'Doctor's Trial' in Nürnberg, which will begin on the
9th December 1946 and, on the 2nd July 1948, will hang dead
from a rope in the prison courtyard. But that is not now.

(As Lina Kretschmar.) Is it now?

HE

Whenever you want.

SHE
No pain?

HE
None.

SHE
No crying?

HE
No.

SHE
Just sleep?

HE
Yes.

SHE
And I'll become a human being again?

HE
We all will.

SHE
(Short pause.) Then it's now.

HE

(Takes out a syringe. It is filled with darkness. To the baby bag.)
It's nothing personal. It's the need for control. It isn't 'He
created the world in his own image'; it's 'He recreated the
world in his own image'. That's the way it is. The need to
alter the letters on your forehead.

*(HE goes over to the baby and removes the quilt. The light shines up
at him with an incredible strength. HE is blinded for a moment, then
he bends down, slips the needle into the child and presses the syringe
down. The light slowly fades.)*

SHE
In the church record book, the cause of death is given as:
Schwäche im Herzen. (Short pause.) Weakness in the heart.

17

There's a furnace some place where the fire never goes out.
Hidden, deep in the darkest woods you can imagine.
Almost invisible. But it's there.

An insatiable fire.

An all-consuming sun.

Its thirst and hunger are all but unstoppable.

It gorges on the smallest toes and tiniest nails. On fused fingers and hare-lips. On the erroneous course of electrons in the brain. It delights in empty pupils and hearts lacking valves. Convulsions of the flesh and a perforated ear drum. It gorges on voices in heads and urine in trousers.

A fire which has always been there, which warms us.

Its name is humanity.

- The end -

A REMARKABLE PERSON
Pernille Dahl Johnsen

This translation was supported by the
Writers' Guild of Norway

Chopin's funeral march is heard, the classic, well-known opening. THE OTHER stands beside an urn. A funeral wreath bearing the words 'Thank you for everything'. The music fades down but can still be heard.

THE OTHER: *(Sadly, to 'the congregation'/the audience.)* She was utterly remarkable. As a person. And as an author. Everybody knew that. But did *she* know?

(To the urn.) Did you know? In your writing– … you had a completely separate world. To begin with, it was difficult to enter, but then it opened up and one was imperceptibly lifted into this strange, magical and yet so recognisable– …

(In tears.) I feel that I found *myself* for the very first time in your books.

THE ONE sits on a bench, drying tears. THE ONE has clearly been listening to the speech. THE OTHER sits down beside THE ONE. They eat Napoleon cake. The music disappears.

THE ONE: This puts everything into perspective, doesn't it? Will anyone speak that way – of *me* – one day?

THE OTHER: *(Nervously to THE ONE.)* All this to do with self-sabotage… I don't understand the phenomenon. That people destroy things *for themselves?*

THE ONE: And unconsciously to boot. That's what's scariest. That's why it has such fatal consequences.

THE OTHER: So how can one protect oneself, if it's unconscious?

THE ONE: The antidote is to know what one wants. There are surprisingly many people who simply aren't clear about that. In life. What *I* want is that when my book is published–

THE OTHER: The book about the Storyteller.

THE ONE: – that *is* a good name for the main character, isn't it?–

THE OTHER: Remarkable.

THE ONE: – when my book is published, I hope the critics realise that I'm– …

THE OTHER: Remarkable?

THE ONE: Sincere. As an author.

They both look at the audience and around the room and stage.

THE OTHER: Look at those flowers. Look at that urn. Look at this place.

THE ONE: Funerals really can be quite– … inspiring.

THE OTHER clears away the plates, they rise, clearly entering a 'different space' – lights up across the whole stage where there are a number of stage set elements. THE ONE looks around.

THE ONE: 'It's like being– … on a stage set!' thought the Storyteller, amazed, looking around. 'Everything in this woman's home is deliberate. Every object a prop, carefully chosen and placed like testimony in a courtroom.' No, not both 'stage set' and 'courtroom'; the critics would just accuse me of mixed metaphors. 'Every object a prop, carefully chosen– … to paint a picture! The function of this home is not to form a framework around a life to be lived but, on the contrary, to frame a portrait of the owner, to be printed on the retina of the observer!'

THE OTHER: Remarkable.

THE ONE: In the third chapter–

THE OTHER: Oh no, the third chapter.

THE ONE: – in the difficult third chapter it's time for my readers to realise that my book concerns them; that they, too, construct glossy images of themselves to make an impression on other people. Isn't home decor the perfect example?

THE OTHER: Home decor is the impossible third chapter example?

THE ONE: What could be more modern-day facadomania than that?

THE OTHER: Facade– …?

THE ONE: Facadomania! That *is* a good word for it, isn't it?

They enter a 'different space' again.

THE ONE/The Trendsetter: I want you to furnish my home in such a way that when people come here and have a look around, they'll immediately get a sense of what kind of person I am.

THE OTHER/The Interior Decorator: You want something trendy?

THE ONE/The Trendsetter: *(Risibly.)* Trendy? Is that your impression; that I'm someone who follows trends? Who does what everyone else is doing? I am an *individual!*

THE OTHER/The Interior Decorator: And thank goodness for that! I just had to test you out.

THE ONE/The Trendsetter: Aaaah…?

THE OTHER/The Interior Decorator: I did a home for this woman a while back and it turned out that she was an artist.

THE ONE/The Trendsetter: No! Artists are supposed to be such eccentrics with their own remarkable taste and then she goes and hires *someone else* to do her home for her? No, poor thing!

THE OTHER/The Interior Decorator: So now I test out all my customers before taking a commission on.

THE ONE grabs the urn and places it on the bench.

THE ONE/The Trendsetter: Of course.

(About the urn.) Here's the Buddha. For the house altar.

(Anxious.) I hope you don't think it smacks a bit too much of– ... touristy– ... Thailand?

THE OTHER/The Interior Decorator: It *is* a bit kind of– ...

THE ONE/The Trendsetter: What?

THE OTHER/The Interior Decorator: Bangkok.

THE ONE/The Trendsetter: So how can you convey that it's actually from Cambodia?

THE OTHER/The Interior Decorator: There are so many people who have been there too now, it's hardly going to make that much of an impression.

THE ONE/The Trendsetter: But this isn't just a cheap souvenir; it's authentic!

THE OTHER/The Interior Decorator: I see. How can we convey that it's authentic without revealing that you *want* to convey it's authentic.

THE ONE/The Trendsetter: Yes, because that would just seem snobbish.

THE OTHER/The Interior Decorator: So: How to convey that you're above cheap, touristy stuff, but all the same not snobbish...

THE ONE/The Trendsetter: And without it looking like I'm trying to decrease the snob value!

THE OTHER/The Interior Decorator: Absolutely; the worst!

THE ONE/The Trendsetter: The wall behind the altar could be papered with a portrait of me.

(Sudden idea.) As a three-year-old!

THE OTHER/The Interior Decorator: As a symbol!

THE ONE/The Trendsetter: Of the authentic *I*. In other words, it's an altar which says…?

THE OTHER/The Interior Decorator: 'I worship *myself*.'

THE ONE/The Trendsetter: You're good.

THE OTHER/The Interior Decorator: The altar shouldn't be placed where people can see it straight away, because then it'll have the opposite effect: 'I don't actually worship myself, I'm just trying to *appear* like someone who does.'

THE ONE/The Trendsetter: *Very* good.

THE OTHER/The Interior Decorator: We'll put the Buddha in your bedroom!

(She places the urn on another stage set element.) There it's clearly not an attempt to show how well-travelled you are,–

THE ONE/The Trendsetter: – because then it would have been in the lounge!

THE OTHER/The Interior Decorator: – but first and foremost it's evidence of your individuality: It really *does* give you personal pleasure; why else would you want it to be the first thing you see every morning?

THE ONE/The Trendsetter: And that's actually true too…

THE OTHER/The Interior Decorator: No!

THE ONE/The Trendsetter: It's *exactly* what gives me the greatest pleasure; of all my things, it's what says *most about me!*

THE OTHER/The Interior Decorator: And best of all: Since it's in your bedroom, and you're in the lounge most of the day–

THE ONE/The Trendsetter: – I won't have to look at it!

They suddenly change mode; it is apparent they have only been playing roles, and now drop them.

THE OTHER: Third chapter example: Check!

THE ONE: No. Too extreme.

THE OTHER: People fill their homes with identity indicators!

THE ONE: People don't hide their trophies away in the bedroom.

THE ONE places the urn back in its original place by the wreath.

THE OTHER: For something to be self-sabotage, then, one has to ruin things for oneself… without realising that is what one is doing?

THE ONE: The antidote is to know what one wants! I want my readers to realise that facadomania can ruin their lives! Not even – *in our own homes!* are we free of this everlasting project.

THE OTHER: That one doesn't simply fail, but actually *sees to it* that one's own chances are ruined?

THE ONE: I need an example! That my readers can identify with.

THE OTHER: That one throws spanners in *one's own works?!*

THE ONE: This book is the most important project of my life! I've got a deadline!

THE OTHER: *(Pulling herself together.)* The task, then, is to find an example of the way in which modern, aware people suffering from fadaco… er, from famado… famaco…

THE ONE: Facadomania. In the first chapter the Storyteller comes face-to-face with the most primitive form of facadomania: What did people do in the old days, to try and make an impression on others?

(Playing a boastful landowner.) 'No one has as much silver on her traditional *bunad* costume as my wife!'

(Back to normal.) They used expensive possessions, didn't they? People don't go round boasting about owning expensive things anymore these days. In the second chapter–

THE OTHER: They don't?

THE ONE: Today what counts is to be 'deep' and have 'heartfelt experiences'. If you go 'Look how wealthy I am', everybody knows you're far too shallow to be deep, and you've lost straight away!

THE OTHER: Ah.

THE ONE: In the second chapter the Storyteller deals with more modern times, where people try and make an impression through what they *are.*

(Playing a pompous academic.) 'I'm an academic. Yes, six years at university.'

(Back to normal.) Today, people don't play the university card anymore. In the third–

THE OTHER: They do!

THE ONE: 'Look at the level of education I've achieved' – it's transparent to everyone you have no self-confidence!

THE OTHER: Ah.

THE ONE: Then they only pity you.

THE OTHER: Ah.

THE ONE: Of course there are people lagging behind who are still carrying on like that–

THE OTHER: Exactly!

THE ONE: – but nobody cares what *they're* doing! I'm talking about aware people! I'm talking *to* aware people; those people are my readers. And so the Storyteller arrives at the notorious third chapter.

Short beat.

THE OTHER: Good title for a book, though, isn't it: Facado– … nemia?

THE ONE: I'm going to have to invent a better word, or the critics will slaughter me.

THE ONE sits down at the bench. Chopin's funeral march is heard. THE OTHER stands sadly by the urn. The light concentrates about the urn.

THE OTHER: *(Sadly to 'the congregation'/the audience.)* She understood human nature. She truly did.

(In tears, to the urn.) In your writing– … You showed us who we are. Thank you.

Lights up on THE ONE, who has clearly been listening; she dries her tears. They eat Napoleon cake. Both sigh, blow their noses and pull themselves together.

THE OTHER: Look at those flowers! What an urn! Isn't it an inspiring place?

THE ONE: That's not the question. The question is: What would people say if they knew I habitually sit at home like this, imagining my own funeral? Could they identify with that?

THE OTHER: Maybe– … not. That's more like something one did when one was ten and felt that nobody cared, so one would go up to one's room and slam the door shut. And when nobody cared about that either, one would imagine one was dead and one's parents stood by one's graveside, crying with regret.

THE ONE: I imagine my own funeral to– … get back at people?

THE OTHER: I guess it's more… like when one puts on a sad film; one needs to cry.

THE ONE: That's what people should say at my funeral: 'She was an inexpressibly sad person.'

THE OTHER: Maybe just a bit sensitive?

THE ONE: 'For an author, she was surprisingly *in*sensitive. So insensitive that it wasn't enough to put on a sad film. To be able to cry, she had to conjure up an image of her own funeral.'

(Short pause.) One thing's for sure: I'm not writing a word about all this to do with funerals!

THE OTHER: I'm not writing a single word!

THE ONE: I'm shutting up about funerals!

THE OTHER: I'm shutting the hell up about funerals!

Beat.

THE ONE: There is of course a biological aspect in facadoman– … er, facade construction. We need to make ourselves attractive to potential mates.

THE OTHER: And then we're flock animals. We need to form bonds with other members of the flock.

THE ONE: We know instinctively that if we get sick or old and don't have any strong bonds with anyone, we risk being left behind when the flock moves on.

THE OTHER: Left to die. Without so much as a funeral.

THE ONE: *(Eager.)* A good facade equals 'Easy to Like': 'Easy to Form Bonds With'! Third chapter example: Check!

THE OTHER: And that's it? So why am I writing about it if the issue's so obvious?

THE ONE: I'm writing about it because people who already *have* a mate, who already *have* children, who are successful, rich, independent of others – they keep on constructing, constructing, constructing their facades! Isn't that something people should be– … thinking about?

THE OTHER: Third chapter: Something for people to be 'thinking about'…

THE ONE: I should at least have an opinion to give. An opinion!

THE ONE sinks down on the bench, but THE OTHER stops her.

THE OTHER: I can't sabotage things now; I've got a deadline here. Humans are, then, flock animals. Humans are constantly driven to *(as if by rote)* form bonds with people, *nurture* the bonds, *strengthen* the bonds, *develop* the bonds– … A cobweb of bonds that we have to keep on checking, repairing, buckling, bracing and blah, blah, blah…

THE ONE: I who was the very epitome of 'A Person With Forceful Opinions' when I was young…

THE OTHER: So what happened to me?

THE ONE: I suddenly woke up one day, in the middle of my twenties, in the middle of a student party, in the middle of a conversation – if one could call it that; I was giving my opinion about something, I hardly did anything else at that time.

THE OTHER plays a young version of 'Her Old Self' at a student party.

88

THE OTHER/Her Old Self: A dialectic approach means we gather all the pigeons together and cart them out of town; they're crapping all over the house facades!

THE ONE: Suddenly it hit me:

THE OTHER/Her Old Self: Do I really mean that? Why? Do I have any personal experience of this opinion matching up with reality?

THE ONE: No.

THE OTHER/Her Old Self: Do I have an opinion of pigeons at all?

THE ONE: No.

THE OTHER/Her Old Self: Have I just... adopted it?!

THE ONE: Yes.

THE OTHER/Her Old Self: Does any one of my opinions actually arise *in me?*

THE ONE: Nope.

THE OTHER/Her Old Self: So then I'm not a very reflective person? Aware?

BOTH: I thought *that* was what I was.

THE OTHER/Her Old Self: I come across as a typical... intellectual. Sexless.

THE ONE: I became afraid! Afraid that my intellectual style made others feel stupid. So I began to make myself–

THE OTHER/Her Old Self: *(Makes herself sweet, innocent, rather fluttery.)* – harmless.

THE ONE: I abandoned my vocabulary–

THE OTHER/Her Old Self: – pretending I'm looking for words so that others have to help me to er... um...

89

THE ONE: – *express* myself.

THE OTHER/Her Old Self: *(Makes herself preoccupied, remote.)* Because I am so… so…

THE ONE: – *preoccupied.*

THE OTHER/Her Old Self: – that I forget– … what I was going to say.

(Back to normal, drily.) It paid off.

THE ONE: It paid off.

THE OTHER: Women got friendlier and men got more interested.

THE ONE: And all my opinions fell powerless and dead to the ground, until one day I had to admit that:

THE OTHER: I don't have an iota of opinion about sweet F.A.

THE ONE: And worse still:

THE OTHER: I feel incapable of deciding about anything.

Beat.

Is there any Napoleon cake left?

BOTH: Should I have more? I can't decide.

THE ONE: Thankfully there's none left.

THE OTHER: I'm really bad at portioning things, too.

THE ONE: I use up the joys of life.

THE OTHER: Me, who has so few of them.

THE ONE: And so seldom.

Beat.

THE ONE: Facade– … obsession?

THE OTHER: What would my readers say if they knew how few I have?

THE ONE: Facade obsessions?

THE OTHER: Opinions. And joys of life.

THE ONE: I'm not writing a word about that side of my personality.

THE OTHER: I'm shutting up about that side of my—

BOTH: – personality!

THE OTHER becomes 'The TV Host'.

THE OTHER/The TV Host: *(To 'the TV show audience'/the audience)* Welcome to *The Culture Show*, where today's topic is: Are people *born* authors or is it something they *become*? To help us answer this question, we've invited to the studio a beloved author who, for over thirty-five years, has been writing award-winning books,–

THE ONE: Oh, could it be...?

THE OTHER/The TV Host: – full of insight into human nature. Our very own, critically acclaimed–

THE THIRD enters the 'TV studio' as 'The Famous Author' and greets 'The TV Host'.

THE ONE: *(Cheering to herself about the 'guest' on the TV-show.)*

Yay!

THE THIRD and THE OTHER sit down, always observing the audience as if they were the TV studio audience. THE ONE watches from the sideline as if watches TV.

THE OTHER/The TV Host: Lovely to have you with us!

THE THIRD/Famous Author: Lovely to be here!

THE OTHER/The TV Host: So, how did you become an author?

THE THIRD/Famous Author: I never did.

THE OTHER/The TV Host: No?

THE THIRD/Famous Author: All my life, I've considered myself to be unemployed, and since I have nothing to do, I amuse myself by writing.

THE ONE: *(To herself about 'The Famous Author'.)* Look what an original personality! She has been writing books full-time for thirty-five years but can still come up with 'I'm not an author' on live TV.

THE OTHER/The TV Host: But what was the first thing that you sat down and wrote, in all seriousness?

THE THIRD/Famous Author: I can't say I've ever done that.

THE ONE: *(Mockingly about 'The Famous Author'.)* 'Look what a genius I am! Writing comes to me so easily and yet I write so supremely well that my books have been winning awards for thirty-five years.'

THE THIRD/Famous Author: I make my debut every time. I'm a beginner with every single book.

THE ONE: And there's the pearl of pearls in the glossy image of this woman.

THE THIRD/Famous Author: 'I'm a beginner with every single book.'

THE ONE: *(To 'the TV show audience'/the audience.)* – actually means: 'Look what risks I take in my authorship! I leap into the unknown without ever knowing if there is somewhere to land on the other side! Look, I'm a true *Homo ludens: THE PLAYING HUMAN!'*

In the following THE THIRD and THE OTHER are unaware of THE ONE, even when she talks to them.

THE THIRD/Famous Author: I feel very humble in having had this book published.

THE OTHER/The TV Host: Of course authors have to fight for readers' attention. Wanting to take up that much space,–

THE OTHER/The TV Host and THE ONE: – is that humility?

THE THIRD/Famous Author: I feel humble for having been allowed this success.

THE OTHER/The TV Host: Isn't it the fact that you're good that has given you success?

THE THIRD/Famous Author: That's for others to judge.

THE OTHER/The TV Host: Let's talk about the book with which you're currently enjoying overnight success,–

THE THIRD/Famous Author: It's not an overnight success for me; I've been working for many years with–

THE OTHER/The TV Host: Exactly! Isn't that why you feel you deserve the success, in terms of effort if nothing else?

THE THIRD/Famous Author: I've been very fortunate in working with excellent publishers,–

THE OTHER/The TV Host: 'Fortunate'? Is *that* the explanation: Luck?

THE THIRD/Famous Author: I'm sorry, isn't this beginning to be a little unpleasant…?

THE OTHER/The TV Host and THE ONE: It's *unpleasant* to say that you're good?

THE ONE circles around 'The Famous Author', who is unaware of her.

THE ONE: When the TV Host has to squeeze it out of you –
no one can accuse you of being boastful, can they?

THE OTHER/The TV Host: Are you scared? That people are
so envious of your success that if you then go and say 'I'm
good, so I deserve it,' that you'll stick in their throats?

THE THIRD/Famous Author: I don't think like that.

THE OTHER/The TV Host: How important is it to you to
come across as a humble person?

THE THIRD/Famous Author: I haven't got the slightest need
to 'come across' as humble.

THE ONE: You've been fighting as if possessed for ten minutes
to avoid saying that you're good?

THE THIRD/Famous Author: I have a relaxed attitude to what
others think about me.

*THE THIRD freezes. THE ONE and THE OTHER laugh heartily.
THE OTHER relinquishes the 'TV Host' role. They wind themselves
up. THE THIRD remains 'frozen' in the following segment.*

THE ONE: Your intro said 'a beloved author'. You're already
loved!

THE OTHER: Did you have to be An Extraordinary
Personality *too*?

THE ONE: Not to mention then trying to come across as
humble?

THE OTHER: When it comes to stuffing the glossy image of
themselves–

THE ONE: – into the heads of others, people are such, such–

THE ONE and THE OTHER: *(Together.)* – VULTURES!

THE ONE: *(Raging.)* You're not sincerely humble!

THE OTHER: You've spent *half your life* getting people to
see you!

THE ONE and THE OTHER: *(Together.)* : *ADMIT IT!!*

*THE ONE and THE OTHER 'wake up' to their own rage and suddenly
calm down completely.*

THE ONE: This example, of my reaction to this author's TV
performance–

THE OTHER: – is not going into the third chapter.

THE ONE: People would just think that I was envious.

THE OTHER: I'm going to keep quiet about it.

THE ONE: I'm going to keep completely quiet about it.

Beat.

THE OTHER: 'Conversation', thought the Storyteller. 'One
might just as well call it 'an exchange of advertising'. One
thinks one is communicating, but actually each person in
turn is simply getting two or three minutes' advertising
space in the mind of the other.'

THE ONE: But what are humans looking for in this eternal
pursuit of attention?

*Only now does THE THIRD break from the frozen position. THE
ONE and THE OTHER are startled.*

THE THIRD/Famous Author: Confirmation. That one is worth
something.

THE ONE: OK: I hereby confirm that you are worth a great
deal to me.

THE THIRD/Famous Author: One doesn't believe it without
reasons.

THE ONE: Because you are so… talented.

THE THIRD/Famous Author: It's not enough.

THE OTHER: I hereby confirm that you are… a good citizen?

THE THIRD/Famous Author: It's not enough.

THE ONE: A good friend, perhaps? A thoroughly good person; no one's as good as you!

THE THIRD/Famous Author: It's not enough.

THE THIRD escorts THE OTHER to stand high up on a stage set element.

I admire you!

THE OTHER: This is somewhere near the mark, I think?

THE ONE: Because if one is admired, one can achieve…?

THE OTHER: Oh, anything's possible!

THE THIRD/Famous Author as Admirer: *(To THE OTHER.)* I'm going to tell the entire publishing industry how brilliantly you write! Especially the book about facado– …?

THE ONE: Facadomania?

THE OTHER: Job opportunities! A career!

THE ONE: Because if one has a career, one can achieve…?

THE OTHER: A more enjoyable life! I'll get invited to parties!

THE OTHER and THE THIRD/Famous Author as Admirer: Cheers!

THE ONE: Where what happens?

THE OTHER: Where– … people laugh at my jokes. *(Immediately in a laughing mood.)* And so the Neurotic Female was to tell a joke.

THE THIRD/Famous Author as Admirer: *(Amused.)* And?

THE OTHER: *(Even more amused.)* And everybody knew she was really funny.

THE THIRD/Famous Author as Admirer: *(Even more amused.)* And?

THE OTHER: *(Barely managing to contain herself.)* So she told the joke,–

THE THIRD/Famous Author as Admirer: *(Barely managing to contain herself.)* And?

THE OTHER: – and then followed up with the punchline!

THE OTHER and THE THIRD crease up in laughter.

THE ONE: And *that*'s what the entire human race is after in its obsessive hunt to make an impression on other people?!

THE OTHER: Now I've got it! Whenever I say something, they listen. People take me seriously!

THE ONE: So what is it I want to say?

THE OTHER: Er… all sorts.

THE ONE: Go on then!

THE OTHER: Erm…

THE THIRD/Famous Author as Admirer: Give us your opinion about things!

THE OTHER: Well, I don't know about opinions exactly…

THE THIRD/Famous Author as Admirer: I read everything about you; I think about you all the time.

THE ONE: Is that admiration enough?

THE OTHER: Not quite.

THE THIRD/Famous Author as Admirer: You really *are* your *self!* I wish I could *be you!*

THE ONE: Golly! What about now then?

THE OTHER: Would you want my thoughts?

THE THIRD/Famous Author as Admirer: Yes!

THE OTHER: Would you want to be inside my mind?

THE THIRD/Famous Author as Admirer: Absolutely!

THE OTHER: Feel as I do?

THE THIRD/Famous Author as Admirer: Yes.

THE OTHER: Have needs like mine?

THE THIRD/Famous Author as Admirer: Yes.

THE OTHER: Or do you really just want to be *your* self but with *my life*?

THE THIRD/Famous Author as Admirer: *(Having to think about it.)* Mmm– … I'd want your life… but I still want to be *my* self.

THE OTHER: NO! IT'S NOT ENOUGH!! You have to want to be ME!

THE ONE: *Why?!*

THE OTHER: Because if people want to be me, it must mean that I'm… A HAPPY PERSON!

Chopin's funeral march. THE THIRD relinquishes the 'Admirer' role, and stands sadly beside the urn.

THE THIRD/Famous Author: *(Sadly to 'the congregation'/the audience.)* I've been constructing a facade for as long as I can remember. It was like I was possessed. I've never had any real conversations with people! But then I read her book about *(concentrates to get the word right, somewhat slower) facadomania*, and realised that when people admired my facade, it wasn't *me* they saw.

(Sobbing.) It was destroying my life, this fadase… this fasame… this fas… fasode…

Enraged.

FASODDING HELL!!

THE THIRD/Famous Author freezes, a raging grimace on her face. Alarmed, THE ONE crosses to THE THIRD to see how ill this daydream has turned out. THE ONE starts wandering.

THE ONE: I either find inspiration now, or the critics are going to slaughter me. Facadocentric?

THE OTHER: Isn't it possible to have a conversation that isn't about selling people something to admire?

THE ONE: More rarely than one thinks.

THE OTHER: Can't I just tell the truth?

THE ONE: Please!

THE OTHER talks to THE THIRD, unaware of her frozen position. THE ONE 'translates' everything THE OTHER says to the audience.

THE OTHER: At the weekend I went for this fantastic ski trip.

THE ONE: 'Look how fit I am!'

THE OTHER: I'm not very fit, so I just went for a short trip; I just wanted to get out in the woods.

THE ONE: 'Look at the contact I have with nature! Such heartfelt experiences!'

THE OTHER: *(To THE THIRD.)* Hi there! I'd like to know who *you* are.

THE THIRD 'wakes up' to answer, but no one's paying her any attention.

THE ONE: 'Look, I'm not at all egocentric!'

THE OTHER: *(To the audience.)* Perhaps I'll abandon this conversation and pretend I'm looking for words so that others'll have to help me to er… um…

THE ONE: – *express* my lack of a personality?

THE OTHER: *(Sincerely to the audience.)* We should teach our children about facadonemia.

THE ONE: Mania.

THE OTHER: Our children shouldn't waste their lives trying to make an impression on others.

THE ONE: 'Look what a caring mother I am!'

THE OTHER: *(Depressed, to THE THIRD.)* I'm going to the bakery to buy some more Napoleon cake. They make the rum cream with real vanilla pods.

THE ONE: 'Look what a lover of good food I am!'

THE OTHER: *(Sincerely to the audience.)* I can't come up with a single thing to say that isn't about being admired.

THE ONE: 'Look how totally honest I am; you can't help liking that!'

THE OTHER: *(To THE ONE.)* That's not why I said it; I just wanted to make contact!

THE ONE: Exactly: The damned facade is just a diversion!

(Discovery.) This has got to go into the manuscript!

THE ONE and THE OTHER: Third chapter example: Check!

THE THIRD climbs up on a stage element.

THE THIRD/Famous Author as Exhibitionist: I'm not hiding it: I *want* to be seen! Regarded as an innovative performance artist!

(Challenging to the audience.) I'll strip naked and masturbate right in people's faces!

THE OTHER: *(Helpfully.)* But haven't we all seen real sex on stage ages ago?

THE THIRD/Famous Author as Exhibitionist: Alright: Then I'll cut myself with knives. Really! Right here and now!

THE OTHER and THE ONE: Why?

THE THIRD/Famous Author as Exhibitionist: I want to show that I take my art seriously.

THE OTHER: But shouldn't that seriousness be expressed in your art?

THE THIRD/Famous Author as Exhibitionist: I don't need your judgment!

THE THIRD starts masturbating.

THE ONE: You do; the judgment you want is 'Look how brave she is!' And then we're right back where we started.

THE THIRD/Famous Author as Exhibitionist: No, because I'm not creating a glossy image! I'm showing exactly what's in here! I expose the nastiest truths about myself!

THE OTHER: *(To THE ONE.)* Apparently we humans have a need to have our identity confirmed?

THE OTHER and THE THIRD/Famous Author: *(THE OTHER calmly illustrating her point, THE THIRD deeply hopeful.)* I hope everyone sees the real me. I hope everyone sees the real me.

THE ONE: And what do humans want with this perpetual confirmation?

THE THIRD/Famous Author as Exhibitionist: I just know I have a compulsion to hang myself from the roof using hooks stuck in my skin. I'm going to hang there and paint innovative– … shit pictures!

THE OTHER: Supposing I confirm your identity as someone who needs to show– … *(enthusiastic idea)* to show themselves off?

(Even more enthusiastic.) You could have the identity of an exhibitionist!

THE THIRD/Famous Author as Exhibitionist: I don't need any labels from you!

THE ONE: No? You'd get your identity confirmed, wouldn't you?

THE THIRD/Famous Author as Exhibitionist: I don't want any kind of 'authorised' mark!

THE OTHER: *(Kindly, helpful.)* I can mark you down as 'non-authorised'?

THE THIRD/Famous Author as Exhibitionist: I refuse to be pigeon-holed!

THE OTHER: *(Kindly, enthusiastic.)* Now I know what identity you can have: A Person Who Did Not Allow Herself To Be Categorised!

THE THIRD/Famous Author as Exhibitionist: Why should you condemn me just because I dare to masturbate in public?

THE ONE and THE OTHER: *(Kindly.)* On the contrary, wank away.

THE THIRD tries some more. Then stops masturbating; she never really got it going anyway.

THE THIRD/Famous Author as Exhibitionist: Exhibitionism is about power. The courage to come forward with your shadowy sides.

THE ONE: 'Look how brave I am!' And straight back to square one. *(To THE OTHER.)* If I publish this book, no one's ever going to want to speak to me. People will feel I'm just sitting there, seeing right through everything they say.

THE ONE and THE OTHER: Third chapter example: Un-check.

THE THIRD/Famous Author as Exhibitionist: I just want to be myself!

THE ONE: So be that! Why is it so damned important that others see it?

THE THIRD/Famous Author as Exhibitionist: OK, then I'll *crap* on the stage! And shove the shit back up my arse afterwards!

(Squats down and starts to strain.) Gnnnn!

THE ONE: Would you say that you realise yourself in your artistic work?

THE THIRD/Famous Author as Exhibitionist: *(Strains.)* Gnnnn!

THE ONE: You *do*, don't you? And what does that mean actually, 'realising yourself'?

THE THIRD/Famous Author as Exhibitionist: *(Strains.)* Gnnnn!

THE ONE: 'To realise' means to bring an idea to reality, yes? So, since it is 'your self' you're supposed to realise, then your 'self' must be an IDEA you have? *So where have you got that idea from?!*

THE ONE challenges THE THIRD to answer. Short pause. THE THIRD takes a deep breath as if to answer, but has nothing more to offer than to strain even harder.

THE THIRD/Famous Author as Exhibitionist: GNNNN!

THE ONE: 'Really? Your motto is simply to *be* yourself?' asked the Storyteller,–

THE ONE is circling around THE THIRD.

THE OTHER: – circling around the poor thing.

THE ONE: '*My* motto is to spend my life tracking down whoever invented '*Just be yourself*' and then to break the neck of the heartless bastard! Just be your *self!* Don't be your own invention, or your dream or your ever-recurring nightmare, no: Just be – *your self!* Who *is* this 'My Self' that I'm supposed to JUST BE?!

THE ONE sits down at a stage element.

THE OTHER: What was it she said, that psychologist…?

THE OTHER now becomes 'The Psychologist' – adult, sympathetic, calmly attentive. THE ONE becomes 'Her Old Tearful Self' – depressed and tearful.

THE ONE/Her Old Tearful Self: *(Tearful.)* I'm so different all the time! I don't know who I really am!

THE OTHER/The Psychologist: I can see this is difficult for you.

THE ONE/Her Old Tearful Self: *(Tearful.)* When I'm at a book launch, I become a critic:

She suddenly becomes 'The Critic' – arrogant and intellectual.

THE THIRD/Famous Author as Exhibitionist: Gnnnn!

THE ONE/The Critic: The book seems very laboured. I think all the author wants to do is defy the critics.

(Her Old Tearful Self again, tearful.) While when I meet an attractive person at a party, I turn into a bimbo:

THE THIRD/Famous Author as Exhibitionist: Gnnnn!

THE ONE plays 'The Fluttery Bimbo', flirts with THE THIRD.

THE ONE/Fluttery Bimbo: What does 'laboured' mean?

(Her Old Tearful Self again, tearful.) And when people talk about their problems, I become a psychologist:

THE THIRD/Famous Author as Exhibitionist: Gnnnn!

THE ONE plays a person exactly like THE OTHER's 'The Psychologist'.

THE ONE/The Psychologist: *(Calmly to THE THIRD.)* I can see this is difficult for you.

(Her Old Tearful Self again, tearful.) People must feel I'm not sincere!

THE OTHER/The Psychologist: But what about you? What do you feel?

THE ONE/Her Old Tearful Self: *(Tearful.)* What?

THE OTHER/The Psychologist: What *do you feel* about all that?

THE ONE/Her Old Tearful Self: *(Tearful.)* I don't know which of them is me!

THE OTHER/The Psychologist: Do you have to choose just one, then?

THE ONE/Her Old Tearful Self: *(Starting, astonished.)* Don't I have to choose just one?

ALL THREE: Don't I have to choose just one?

THE THIRD now relinquishes 'The Famous Author' role, and THE OTHER 'The Psychologist' role.

THE THIRD: *(Confused.)* I thought I had to?

THE ONE/Her Old Tearful Self: *(Confused.)* I thought it was to do with finding One's True Self? One's identity?

ALL THREE: Good God, I thought *that* was what everyone was doing?!

THE ONE relinquishes the 'Her Old Tearful Self' role. They all give an entertaining and theatrical song-and-dance-lecture.

THE ONE: All the '*Find Your Self*' books that make psychologists a fortune?

THE THIRD: All the political decisions based on consideration for someone's identity?

ALL THREE: Complete waste of time.

THE ONE: And the psychologists have known for ages!

THE OTHER: But it fitted our time so well!

THE THIRD: With this enormous surplus of time and energy–

THE ONE: – coupled with an almost total lack of purpose and meaning–

THE OTHER: – everyone suddenly had a project:

ALL THREE: I want to realise myself!

THE ONE: More and more people tried to find something to realise. Two or three years of this realisation equals:

THE OTHER: Angst!

THE THIRD: Which in turn equals:

THE OTHER: Eureka! I have to go to a psychologist!

THE THIRD: Steadily more of our fictitious 'myselfs' became visible to steadily more people. Two or three years of this exposure equals:

THE OTHER: Angst!

THE THIRD: Which in turn equals:

THE OTHER: Eureka! I have to go to a psychologist again!

THE ONE: And that's how we created the idea that humans need an identity.

THE OTHER: And this idea's been allowed to blow itself up into one gigantic hot-air balloon.

THE THIRD: And before the wise – who always knew better – managed to fasten the guy ropes, everyone had bought tickets for the balloon ride.

THE ONE and THE OTHER 'climb on board' onto a stage set element.

Up went the balloon,–

The 'balloon' lifts off; they lose their balance.

THE ONE and THE OTHER: *(Shouting elatedly.)* Whoooaaahh!

THE THIRD: – and The Great Delusion was a fact.

She 'climbs on board' too.

We float around, crying at the top of our voices to the heavens:

ALL THREE: WHO AAAAAAAM I?

THE ONE: WHAAAT?

THE OTHER: WHO *AAAAM* I?

THE ONE: NO: WHO AM *IIII!*

ALL THREE: *(Together through cupped hands to all directions.)* HELLOOOO? WHO AM IIIIII?

Chopin's funeral march is played. THE ONE stands sadly beside the urn. THE THIRD and THE OTHER sit on the bench, listening. All three are wearing mourning veils.

THE ONE: *(Sadly to 'the congregation'/the audience.)* I have been looking for my 'self' as long as I can remember. I was obsessed about having an identity. But then I read her book about facadonemia– … fadaso… er, fasamo…

THE ONE looks at THE OTHER and THE THIRD squirming embarrassed on the bench. THE ONE faces 'the congregation'/audience again, rescuing herself.

(Tearfully, to the urn.) – but then I read your life-changing book – especially that wonderful third chapter about obsessive facade construction – and realised that while I was hunting about for a 'me' for people to admire, my whole life was passing me by!

(Breaks down in tears, grabs the urn.) I have this remarkable author to thank for my escaping MY SELF!

THE THIRD and THE OTHER sit shamefaced on the bench. They whisper to each other under their breath.

THE THIRD: Isn't it somewhat alarming that *I* should sit at home and get carried away with my future funeral?

THE OTHER: People need a release; some go jogging.

THE THIRD: But all the farewell speeches are about how fantastic I was. Doesn't that reek of facado–

THE ONE: The realities! In the third chapter I want to write about the physical realities of human life.

THE ONE, THE OTHER and THE THIRD throw their veils on the floor. They put on a lecture, illustrating as they go.

THE OTHER: Situation A: I sit on a bench at a bus stop eating Napoleon cake.

THE ONE sits down on the bench and starts eating Napoleon cake.

People walk past, glancing at me as they go.

THE THIRD goes past, glancing at THE ONE.

The cake tastes fantastic:

THE ONE: The Lovely Yellow – mmmmh!

THE OTHER: Situation B: My face is disfigured.

THE ONE becomes 'Disfigured', pulling an ugly grimace, and remains so for the rest of the scene.

THE OTHER (CONT'D): I eat cake on the bench, people glance at me and look away again when they see I'm disfigured.

THE THIRD walks past, sees THE ONE/Disfigured. THE ONE/ Disfigured smiles amicably, THE THIRD looks at her in horror and then looks away. Walks back to THE OTHER.

THE OTHER (CONT'D): People don't talk to me. But when they have to, they're unable to look into my eyes.

THE THIRD becomes 'Person with Fluttering Gaze' and walks over to THE ONE/Disfigured, who smiles friendly. THE THIRD's gaze fluttering.

THE THIRD/Person with Fluttering Gaze: Excuse me, do you know if the bus has gone?

THE ONE/Disfigured: *(Has difficulties talking owing to the disfigurement.)* Yes, it has.

THE THIRD/Person with Fluttering Gaze: OK.

THE ONE/Disfigured: And there's no train. And no plane. And no boat. So everything in your life is too late.

THE THIRD/Person with Fluttering Gaze: *(Smiles falsely.)* OK, thank you very much.

THE ONE/Disfigured stares, hurt, at THE THIRD/Person with Fluttering Gaze.

THE OTHER: How *does* the Napoleon cake taste?

*THE THIRD relinquishes the 'Person with Fluttering Gaze' role.
THE ONE/Disfigured rediscovers the cake, bites a piece off, chews
in astonishment.*

THE ONE/Disfigured: *(Astonished and happy.)* The Lovely
Yellow!

THE OTHER: *(Triumphantly.)* The realities! If we humans
are to be happy, we must relate to the *physical, perceptible*
REALITIES! – and not whatever picture of us other
people might have in their heads.

THE THIRD: Did I just give an opinion?

THE OTHER: And in the very third chapter!

THE OTHER and THE THIRD: Double-check!

THE ONE/Disfigured: *(To herself, inhaling the smell. Difficult to
speak owing to the disfigurement. Looks at the 'pigeon'/the urn.)*
Look at the pigeons! Grey? Pigeons are green and pink
and purple! Have I ever looked a bird right in the eyes?

*(She lies down with her head on the floor to come to the pigeons'
eye-height.)* Hello, you! Your eyes are on the side of your
head, one on each side!

(Picks up the 'pigeon'/the urn in her hand, kneels.) So if I'd been on
the other side of you, you'd see me *there* with your *other* eye?

*THE THIRD becomes 'Disfigured', too, kneels down on the other side
of the 'pigeon'. Both stare fascinated at the 'pigeon' from either side.*

THE THIRD/Disfigured: *(To the 'pigeon'/the urn.)* Hello? Don't
be afraid! I'm not the least bit dangerous.

*THE ONE/Disfigured and THE THIRD/Disfigured lift their heads
and their respective gazes so they look each other straight in the face.
They stare into each other's eyes, both still disfigured.*

THE ONE/Disfigured and THE THIRD/Disfigured: Pigeons are some pretty crazy creatures! If people could see me now, they'd think I was mad.

THE OTHER: *And what of it?* It doesn't make any difference what others might think about me! *The realities!*

THE ONE/Disfigured and THE THIRD/Disfigured: Yes, *that's* right, yes!

THE OTHER: It could even be interesting.

THE OTHER becomes 'Cold Person on the Street', sits down on a stage set element. Looks nervously at the crazy, disfigured woman and turns away. THE ONE/Disfigured and THE THIRD/Disfigured talk to the 'pigeon'.

THE THIRD/Disfigured: And this is where you live.

THE ONE/Disfigured: On the lowest of the lowest rungs and, presumably, with no depth of vision!

THE ONE/Disfigured and THE THIRD/Disfigured: *(To THE OTHER/Cold Person on the Street.)* Do you know why we humans have depth of vision?

THE OTHER/Cold Person on the Street: *(Coldly, unwilling.)* Do you mind, I'm just sitting here waiting for the bus.

THE ONE/Disfigured: Yes, but I've got two eyes that look at one and the same thing from slightly different angles: While my right eye sees more of the object's right side–

THE THIRD/Disfigured: – my left sees more of the object's left side.

THE ONE/Disfigured: Together I can see that the object doesn't just have a facade. Which equals:

THE ONE/Disfigured and THE THIRD/Disfigured: Objects have depth! – equals depth of vision.

THE OTHER/Cold Person on the Street: I've never thought about it.

THE ONE/Disfigured: This pigeon might think that you're a one-dimensional individual–

THE ONE/Disfigured and THE THIRD/Disfigured: – but I can see that you're much more than the facade you're wearing today.

THE OTHER/Cold Person on the Street: *(Astounded.)* The facade I'm wearing today?!

THE THIRD/Disfigured puts the urn back in place by the funeral wreath.

THE THIRD/Disfigured: And that's how I could have started completely different conversations with people!

THE ONE/Disfigured and THE THIRD/Disfigured sit down at the same stage set element and 'get on the same wavelength' with THE OTHER/Cold Person on the Street in a soundless conversation. A few bars of a different, less well-known part of Chopin's funeral march than we've heard so far while they 'talk'. The music fades down. THE ONE/Disfigured and THE THIRD/Disfigured relinquish their 'Disfigured' role.

THE ONE: *(Sudden idea, to THE THIRD.)* And after a life-long friendship, this person would come to my funeral and say…

Chopin's funeral march, the classic opening as before. THE OTHER/Cold Person on the street walks to the urn.

THE OTHER/Cold Person on the Street: *(Sadly to 'the congregation'/the audience.)* I met her on the street. She was lying down talking to a pigeon.

(To the urn.) Thank you for being so remarkable. Both as a person and as an author. Your third chapter showed me that I wasn't really here! In the physical realities! I wasn't living!

She throws her arms tearfully about the urn.

I am NOT ALIIIIIIVE!

THE OTHER/Cold Person on the Street freezes. THE THIRD crosses towards THE OTHER and thoughtfully regards the melodramatic daydream.

THE THIRD: 'I look around me inside this daydream and understand immediately who I am,' said the Storyteller, facing a decisive choice: 'I must either leave my storytelling behind me for good, or I will be forced to tell the truth.'

Sarcastic about the daydream.

'Look, the church is full to the brim with mourners! Surely that must mean I was enormously well-liked. So I've fulfilled my *real* life project: Living to be able to die with a good reputation.'

THE OTHER relinquishes the 'Cold Person on the Street' role.

THE OTHER: I know what is meant by self-sabotage. Self-sabotage is when two wills exist within me.

She hands out mourning veils to THE ONE and THE THIRD.

Let the battle begin!

THE ONE and THE THIRD whip each other, using the mourning veils as if they were wet towels one can fling out and withdraw very fast, thus whipping/hurting others.

THE THIRD: I have to make a decision! The deadline is just around the corner!

THE ONE: I can't let on that I daydream about my own funeral!

THE THIRD: It's the funerals that I have to write about. Am I to reveal the truth behind everyone else's facade and not my own?

THE ONE: No critic would take me seriously.

THE THIRD: It's precisely in that they will take me seriously! I stand naked before them.

THE ONE: Like someone who daydreams about ultimate admiration.

THE THIRD: Like someone who knows what she's writing about!

THE ONE: Like someone who feels sorry for herself!

THE THIRD: Like someone who really knows herself. *(She gets in a really good blow.)*

I win!

THE OTHER: 'I' have destroyed things for 'Me' equals:

THE THIRD and THE ONE: Self-sabotage? Not at all: I've just finally become *(triumphantly to the audience)* MY SELF!!

ALL THREE: *(Triumphantly to the audience.)* One of the most aware of all!

They celebrate by eating Napoleon cake. THE ONE becomes 'Freud'.

THE ONE/Freud: The will to pleasure! That's the driving force for man!

THE THIRD: – thought Freud.

THE ONE relinquishes the 'Freud' role, THE OTHER becomes 'Adler'.

THE OTHER/Adler: Twaddle! The driving force for man is the will to power!

THE ONE: – thought Adler.

THE OTHER relinquishes the 'Adler' role, THE THIRD becomes 'Frankl'.

THE THIRD/Frankl: Tripe!

THE OTHER: – thought Frankl. He had survived the horrors of the concentration camp and hence had no patience with either twaddle or tripe.

THE THIRD/Frankl: What characterises man is the will to meaning. To find meaning, that's what we need.

THE THIRD relinquishes Frankl, becomes 'The Critic', goes to the urn. Two bars of Chopin's funeral march; THE ONE and THE OTHER put their plates down and rush to the bench.

THE THIRD/Critic: *(Formally to 'the congregation'/the audience.)* I have been given the task of saying a few words on behalf of the Critics' Association.

THE ONE and THE OTHER look excitedly at each other, looking forward to it.

THE THIRD/Critic (CONT'D): It has been somewhat difficult for us critics to summon up interest in an author who does nothing but sit at home, imagining her own funeral and feeling sorry for herself. Now that she is dead, poor thing, and we are all gathered here to fulfil her ultimate daydream, I can say it straight out:

(To the urn.) You should have stopped feeling sorry for yourself; maybe then both your books and your life would have been completely– … OK.

THE ONE: *(Defensive.)* 'Pity' equals suffering.

THE OTHER: *(Defensive.)* In the sense of 'suffering with someone'.

THE ONE: *(Defensive.)* Exactly!

THE OTHER: You can *feel* with someone and, in the same way, you can *suffer* with someone.

THE ONE: *Exactly!* Pity simply means *empathy!*

THE OTHER: Exactly!

THE ONE: Obviously!!

THE OTHER: Completely!!

THE ONE: And not one single person could venture to say that empathy is anything negative.

THE OTHER: Not one single person!

THE ONE: On the contrary, it's all about *being* empathetic!!

THE OTHER: Exactly!!

Both are terribly angry now; they can barely hold back their rage.

THE ONE: *(Stifled anger.)* Therefore: Can anyone in the world,–

THE OTHER: *(Stifled anger.)* – anybody in Heaven's name,–

THE ONE: – explain to me why everybody agrees that–

THE ONE and THE OTHER: – *self-pity is so terribly WRONG?!*

THE OTHER: 'You thought I was a timid person at the mercy of the critics' verdict over my work,'

THE ONE: – snarled the Storyteller.

THE OTHER: 'The truth is I *don't give a damn* about your verdict!'

THE ONE: If I write that in the third chapter, what will your verdict be then?

THE THIRD/Critic: 'Look how *independent* this author is! Goodness! How *free*, how *remarkable!*'

THE OTHER: 'The truth,'–

THE ONE: – admitted the Storyteller,–

THE OTHER: – 'is that all I want to do with the book is predict any objections the critics could be imagined having, and then rewrite it before they have a chance to open their mouths!'

THE ONE: I hope people understand how much it's cost me to be so utterly sincere?

THE THIRD/Critic: *(To 'the congregation'/the audience.)* All the author wants to achieve with her book, *The Storyteller*, is to convince us that she is one of the few people on earth who isn't engaged in facade construction. The way I see it, she does this simply to further construct her facade as 'A Person Brimming Over with Self-Awareness'.

THE THIRD becomes herself. THE ONE walks over to the left.

THE ONE: I'm going to stop writing!

THE OTHER and THE THIRD run after THE ONE.

THE OTHER and THE THIRD: No, no; that would be self-sabotage!!

THE THIRD: I'll convert the book into an absurd theatre piece about a Storyteller,–

THE OTHER: – and then show it to a handful of people over two or three Performances,–

THE OTHER and THE THIRD: – no one goes to the theatre anymore, do they?

THE ONE: *(About the audience.)* These white wine-drinking theatre people; am I supposed to expose myself to them?! They'd just sit in the auditorium, thinking to themselves:

THE OTHER and THE THIRD become 'Audience Members' with 'glasses of white wine'.

THE OTHER/Audience Member: Oh, the poor thing who's written this must be having such a difficult time with herself.

THE THIRD/Audience Member: Go to a psychologist; get some help mending that there self-image of yours.

THE OTHER/Audience Member: 'Who am I?' *Am* I or *aren't* I, that's the question! Stop giving a damn about all this to-do with identity!

THE THIRD/Audience Member: For my part, I don't in the least care what others think about me!

THE OTHER/Audience Member: I've grown out of that a long time ago!

THE ONE: Equals:

THE OTHER/Audience Member and THE THIRD/Audience Member: *(Self-assuredly to each other.)* I don't do facade construction! *(Suddenly frightened, to the audience.)* Did everyone get that?

THE ONE: I'm going to pick those bastards apart quicker than they can say 'identity crisis'!

THE OTHER and THE THIRD relinquish their role.

THE THIRD: *(Panicking.)* I suppose I could tone down the revelations about myself?

THE OTHER: *(Panicking.)* And excel instead with linguistic– … curiosities?

THE OTHER and THE THIRD say the following simultaneously, but they say different versions; 'mania' and 'nemia', then discover this, and switch – also simultaneously.

THE OTHER	THE THIRD
After all, I just invented the word 'facadomania'. Nemia?	After all, I just invented the word 'facadonemia'. Mania?

THE OTHER and THE THIRD (CONT'D): I'm going to stop writing.

THE ONE: – decided the Storyteller, just before the deadline ran out.

THE OTHER and THE THIRD look at each other in terror.

THE OTHER and THE THIRD: I must ask for help!

THE OTHER and THE THIRD try to force THE ONE to come with them to the edge of the stage.

THE ONE: – raged the Storyteller, as she forced herself to the edge of the stage to cry for help. But what was going to happen when she got there: What was she going to want?

They reach the edge of the stage. THE OTHER and THE THIRD stare at THE ONE, who stares at the audience.

The Storyteller eagerly awaited her next move. Suddenly, she went for it and shouted:

THE OTHER and THE THIRD: *(Hollering at the top of their voices to the audience.)* HEEEEEEELP!

THE ONE: *(To the audience.)* I'M GOING TO HAVE TO WRITE UNDER A PSEUDONYYYYM!

They collapse onto the floor. Pause.

THE OTHER: Since self-sabotage takes place on an *unconscious* level, one can't be too certain that one isn't doing it? Am I just horsing about to avoid writing?

THE ONE: Avoid writing?! *Do I want to avoid writing?!*

THE THIRD: I don't want to want to avoid writing; I want to
be pitied!

*Chopin's funeral march, the hefty and sad part, while they act out
something overly melodramatic, like a mock opera with hefty crying.
THE OTHER suddenly 'wakes up', relinquishing the opera, and the
music abruptly stops.*

THE OTHER: If there's some kind of distressing saboteur
woman in my subconscious,–

THE ONE and THE THIRD: *(Terrified.)* A sabotage– … tress?!?!

THE OTHER: – who's trying to stop me finishing the third
chapter against my will,–

THE ONE and THE THIRD: – *then she's not going to win!*

ALL THREE: *NO SODDING WAY!*

*THE OTHER becomes 'The TV Host', THE THIRD 'The Critic'.
They all go to the 'TV studio'.*

THE OTHER/The TV Host: *(To 'the TV show audience'/the
audience.)* Welcome to *The Culture Show,* where authors get
to meet their critics face to face.

THE THIRD/The Critic: The book is full of confessions of
the most revolting truths about yourself. Why should we
bother wandering this desert of exhibitionism where every
oasis of identity is nothing but a mirage?

THE ONE: I'm extremely humble to have been allowed to
publish this book.

THE THIRD/The Critic: Wanting to take up that much space –
is that humility?

THE ONE: I'm one of the few who have actually understood
what humility is!

THE THIRD/The Critic: So why can't you just be humble? Why is it so damned important that others see it?

THE OTHER/The TV Host: And moving swiftly on...

THE THIRD/The Critic: Doesn't your suffering writer's block so often stem from the fact that, deep down, you've got nothing you want to say?

THE ONE: *(Frightened.)* Nothing I want to say...?

Two bars of Chopin's funeral march. THE THIRD becomes the 'Audience Member' once again.

THE THIRD/Audience Member: *(To 'the congregation'/the audience.)* I have struggled to determine how I was to describe her today at this funeral. She was a completely nondescript individual. Both as a person and as an author. Especially in that nonsensical third chapter.

Back to the 'TV studio'. THE THIRD becomes 'The Critic' once again.

THE ONE: *(To THE THIRD/The Critic, protesting against the horror scenario we have just witnessed.)* Ah-ah-ah! I *do want–* ... to achieve something with this book!

THE THIRD/The Critic: We're all ears...

THE OTHER/TV Host: Go on!

THE ONE: *(Goes for it.)* I want people to be so shaken by what I show them that they collapse! On the spot! And take stock of themselves and their lives.

'The TV Host' and 'The Critic' look at each other in astonishment.

THE THIRD/The Critic: *(Sarcastic.)* The perfect model of humility.

THE OTHER/TV Host: And what are they supposed to do? With themselves and their lives?

THE ONE: How do I know! Can't I point out a flaw in the system without having to have a solution? One person doesn't need to have the answer! We're all colleagues. Aren't we?

THE THIRD/The Critic: Who are colleagues?

THE ONE: Humanity.

THE OTHER and THE THIRD relinquish their role. All three are dumbstruck by the grandiosity. They stand and start walking about in confusion; they become gradually more frenetic during what follows.

THE OTHER: I don't seem too intellectual now, do I?

THE THIRD: It doesn't matter what other people think! I've at least agreed with myself about that!

THE OTHER and THE ONE: *(Relieved.)* Yes, *that's* right, yes.

THE OTHER: *(Walks on, then stops.)* But people will be afraid of me! Do I have to be lonely for the rest of my life?!

THE ONE: I only need to admit something pathetic about myself in the third chapter and HEY PRESTO!–

THE THIRD: – I'm completely harmless! Then people will just feel sorry for me – superb!

THE ONE and OTHER: *(Relieved.)* Yes, *that's* right, yes.

They walk on.

THE THIRD: *(Stops.)* Eureka!!

THE ONE and THE OTHER stop, turn around and look at THE THIRD.

The fact that I'm scared of being too intellectual means of course 'I'm scared'; thus I'm completely harmless! People love stuff like that!

THE ONE and THE OTHER: *(Together, joyful.)* YES! *That's* right, yes!

THE OTHER: I don't *need* to be scared of being too intellectual!

THE ONE: *(Panic-stricken, to THE OTHER.)* On the contrary, that's precisely what I must be: Scared!

THE THIRD: NO!! Listen: I mustn't care about the intellect! As long as *it appears that I fear it,* then everything's OK.

THE OTHER and THE ONE: YES! *That's right, yes!*

All three start.

THE ONE: I know what I want!

ALL THREE: I want to go to a psychologist!

THE THIRD becomes 'The Psychologist'; gives a sympathetic greeting.

THE THIRD/The Psychologist: *(Friendly.)* Welcome!

THE ONE and THE OTHER: *(Distant.)* Yes.

THE THIRD/The Psychologist: Please, sit down.

THE ONE and THE OTHER: *(Distant.)* Yes.

All three sit down.

THE THIRD/The Psychologist: How can I help?

THE ONE: I don't want to publish my book. If people read it, they'll think I'm sitting there seeing right through their facade the whole time. And then no one's ever going to want to speak to me.

(Three-four second pause. Frantically.) Why won't you say anything? Don't you want to speak to me?

Two bars of Chopin's funeral march.

THE ONE: 'Sometimes I want to say seven words,' counted the Storyteller to herself while standing utterly alone at her own funeral. 'Sometimes only three: The third chapter.'

THE OTHER: Freud thought he saw a death wish in our propensity to flee from reality into fiction.

THE ONE: This is love of life! Life is never meaningless as long as one has a facade to polish up!

THE OTHER: I'm inclining towards the death wish.

THE ONE: If I wanted to die, I'd make sure I did die. I wouldn't come up with threats beforehand.

THE OTHER: Threats are not a death wish; they're a cry for help.

ALL THREE: *(To the audience.)* Help! Why do I sit at home imagining my own funeral?

Music – BEIRUT's 'The Gulag Orkestar' as they put all the stage set elements together. It turns out to be a gigantic coffin. Exhausted, THE ONE and THE THIRD fall asleep on top of the coffin. THE OTHER is nowhere to be seen. Music fades out. Knocking sounds. THE ONE and THE THIRD leap up, scared out of their wits. They cling to each other on top of the coffin.

THE ONE: Angst has a *function!* That's what I have to remember. That's why one should never try to get rid of one's angst. One must ask it what it wants.

THE knocking sound again.

THE THIRD: My instinct says 'Flee!'–

THE ONE: I won't get rid of my angst that way.

THE THIRD: – or 'Fight!'

THE ONE: Open the door!

The lid of the coffin opens.

THE OTHER/Angst: *(From inside the coffin.)* All I want from my book is to get back at people.

THE ONE: Slam the door in the face of angst! *(THE THIRD closes the coffin lid again.)*

– and the angst just comes on back.

Renewed knocking on the underside of the lid from inside the coffin.

THE ONE: Barricade the door!

THE THIRD lays her weight on the coffin lid.

– and the angst will climb in the window.

THE OTHER/Angst opens the coffin lid from the foot end and comes half-way out.

THE THIRD: *(Panicking.)* WHAT SHALL I DO?!

THE ONE: Let it in!

THE THIRD holds up the coffin lid; THE OTHER climbs up, scared.

THE OTHER/Angst: I'm looking forward to showing people how hollow and unhappy they are.

THE ONE: Let the angst come right into my lounge.

THE OTHER/Angst backs towards the head end where THE ONE and THE THIRD are. They are terrified.

THE THIRD: *(To THE OTHER/Angst.)* Have a seat, I'm just going to go to my bedroom and relax for a couple of weeks.

THE THIRD sneaks past THE OTHER/Angst and lies down at the foot end of the coffin.

THE ONE: Let the Angst come right into my bedroom,–

THE OTHER/Angst goes to THE THIRD.

THE ONE (CONT'D): – right into my bed.

THE OTHER/Angst lies down behind THE THIRD, closely encircling her.

THE THIRD: Spit it out, you bastard!

THE OTHER/Angst: If people really are that unhappy, then I'm just having a ball kicking those who are down.

THE THIRD: *(To THE OTHER/Angst.)* You damned–

THE ONE: No-no-no!

THE THIRD: *(To THE OTHER/Angst.)* What do you want by saying that?

THE ONE: Excellent!!

THE OTHER/Angst: I don't have the right to publish anything, because I'm not doing it out of love.

THE THIRD: Noted.

THE ONE: *(To THE OTHER/Angst.)* Then everything should be fine?

THE OTHER/Angst: But of course I'm not writing for the critics. I'm writing for *people!* And when *people* get my book in their lap, they're going to be speechless.

THE THIRD sits up.

THE THIRD: *(Hopefully.)* I think it's working, all this to-do with letting the angst in!

THE OTHER/Angst: No one knows what to say…

THE ONE: *(Hopefully.)* Really?

THE OTHER/Angst: – because they *pity me so deeply* for having written something so *banal!*

Short pause. THE OTHER relinquishes the 'Angst' role. Defeated, they all sit down on the coffin together.

THE OTHER: And this obsessive urge to confess?! What do I want to get out of this public-private muck-raking?

Two bars of Chopin's funeral march; THE ONE comes down onto the floor.

THE ONE: *(About the coffin, to 'the congregation'/the audience.)* Blow me, what a person she was! Imagine, she even had *(it turns out that she is not angry)* sufficient integrity to admit to the unsympathetic sides of herself?

THE OTHER: *(Despairing.)* Admiration again.

THE THIRD: No: I want to show my fellow man the way out of facadomania! And it's not just yet another confession: Afterwards I'm going to *forgive myself* publicly too.

THE OTHER: *(Hopeful recognition.)* Oh! So that everyone can see I'm at peace with it all?

THE THIRD: Exactly: That one can find peace in one's soul simply by being sincere.

THE ONE: And then no one will realise that I'm still ashamed!

ALL THREE: THEN I'LL HAVE WON!!

Triumphant music. They walk in a victory parade around the coffin. The music and the three of them suddenly come to an abrupt stop.

THE OTHER: Maybe exhibitionism doesn't have anything to do with a pathological need for attention? Maybe it's just an attempt to free oneself from a false facade?

THE THIRD: One shows the ugly truth about oneself once and for all, so it's impossible to construct a glossy image again?

THE ONE: Maybe one just wants to stop lying?!

They sit down together at the foot end of the coffin. They address the audience.

THE OTHER: For others to have a good impression of me,–

THE THIRD: – is so important to me,–

THE ONE: – because I don't feel secure in myself.

THE OTHER and THE THIRD: Exactly.

THE ONE: To be able to feel secure in myself, I must go inside myself and make peace with what I find there. What I find in there is a simple, single desire:

THE OTHER and THE THIRD: I want others to have a good impression of me.

ALL THREE: *(Amazed with the discovery, together.)* I really *am* to be pitied…!?

THE ONE: As the psychologist explained:

THE THIRD: 'People who don't learn to love themselves at an early age, seldom manage to feel love for themselves as adults either.'

THE OTHER: I'll wind up as a black hole. Which can never be filled.

THE ONE: An infinitely stark, infinitely dark, black hole.

THE ONE, THE OTHER and THE THIRD then crawl down into the coffin. The coffin lid closes. Lights fade.

TIME WITHOUT BOOKS
Lene Therese Teigen

This translation was supported by the
Writers' Guild of Norway

To Cecilia

Situation

TIME WITHOUT BOOKS concerns a country where there was once dictatorship. Now, democracy has been reinstated. What can one speak of after such a national trauma? What is it best to keep quiet about? For whom – and why? There is a shopping centre that was formerly a prison and a new generation that has no idea that that is the case. There are parents who want to give their children a happy life, without agreeing upon what that actually means, and there are children who want to understand why their parents have never spoken about how they feel. How personal is a memory?

Acting Style

TIME WITHOUT BOOKS is written with direct communication with the audience in mind, and for four actors. If preferable, more actors may be used.

Sometimes the actors are themselves on stage; this is a kind of base line in their performance. Taking four actors as read, I use the designations "WOMAN 1", "WOMAN 2", "WOMAN 3" and "MAN" in the manuscript as terms for the actors when it is intended that they are at this performance level. From this base line, where they are closest to themselves, they make comments, watch some of the action, perhaps making notes of what happens and what is said, and glide in and out of the various persons and situations they are portraying. This provides opportunities for improvisation and variation. This base line is also applicable for the third scene, the interrogation scene. Within limits that should be agreed beforehand, the actors may improvise new questions and answers in order to sense the here-and-now situation that every theatre performance actually is.

Characters

Woman 1: SOFIA, TATIANA, LYDIA
Man: PEDRO, ENRIQUE, HECTOR
Woman 2: RITA, YOUNG LYDIA, DAUGHTER
Woman 3: IRENE, AURORA, MARIA, EVA

Character Constellations

- RITA, her mother, SOFIA, and her father, PEDRO. RITA's friends IRENE and TATIANA. In this family, both parents were imprisoned during the period of dictatorship. They later lived in exile in a country far away, where they met each other and had their daughter, RITA. They moved back to their home country when democracy was restored. RITA has acquired new friends in her parents' homeland. We meet her at fourteen, at nineteen and at thirty.
- LYDIA and her husband, ENRIQUE, their daughter AURORA, and LYDIA when young. ENRIQUE was imprisoned when their daughter was one year old. The mother was only young and left quite alone with the daughter, while her husband was in prison.
- MARIA. She was imprisoned during the period of dictatorship.
- HECTOR, EVA and their DAUGHTER. HECTOR was in the military during the period of dictatorship. His wife, EVA, was unable to have children so HECTOR obtained a daughter for them. THE DAUGHTER does not speak.

The Space

It is light, almost white, and there is a white chair in a white dream, and there are no walls here in the dream, just a kind of landscape that stretches away like an open, endless, smooth expanse; it is exactly like it is neither inside nor outside, neither firm nor fleeting. As if everything is changing from something other to something other.

Shared Actions

During the scenes, the participants find paper, from cigarette boxes for example, and write on it. They write with tiny handwriting on thin slips of paper such as paper for making roll-ups or the thin paper that surrounds the cigarettes inside the packet. Generally speaking, what they write down is what is said during the performance so that it may be remembered thereafter. The audience is to be given the sheets and, in the end, is to decide if they should be thrown or forgotten or made publicly available.

The Handmade Jersey

YOUNG LYDIA knits. First a jersey for her daughter AURORA's teddy bear. Later on, the bear gets to wear the jersey. Then she knits an identical child's jersey that she completes during the performance. There is also to be a further jersey of the same kind that AURORA wears right at the end – as if she is wearing the child's jersey, that time has spooled backwards, and her body has become smaller.

The Music

Tango may be exchanged for other rhythms – or not be so very tango-like. Regardless: no show-off tango!

The Text

To suggest a beat or pause in the text, one / indicates a brief pause, and two // indicates a longer one.

1. I Remember

A girl dressed as a bride slowly spins upon her own axis – a music-box dream. This is RITA.

Suddenly, a woman and a man are also in the landscape. All spin slowly, as if each in their own dream – in their own world of memory – and oblivion. They move slowly, limited by what their bodies allow, what is possible with the wounds that they carry. The movements speak of sensuality and longing but they are nevertheless introspective; they are each in their own inner world.

WOMAN 1 moves purposefully towards the audience; she is holding a small roll of paper wrapped in plastic, shows it to the audience.

WOMAN 1: I remember –

But then it is like her energy implodes for she has no words, it stops.

MAN: What?

She looks at the man, as if for help, then back at the audience.

WOMAN 1: *(A new attempt.)* I remember –

She holds the plastic roll up towards the audience, then her eyes. Again it seems as if she wants to say something but just cannot get it out. The MAN comes up. WOMAN 1 gives him the roll, then sits down in the audience. The MAN shows the plastic roll to the audience.

MAN: I remember –

Then nothing more – ceremoniously, as if it is a ritual, he puts down the roll where it is visible to the audience. The bride spins slowly.

THE BRIDE/RITA: *(Spin and stops, spins and stops.)*

I remember… nothing… nothing… nothing.

My mum and dad haven't told me anything,

just that they were in prison because they believed in
something else –

Nothing more.

And I can see, see, see that there's more,

But what can I say?

I'm engaged.

We'll be married soon, have children, our own family.

Have to clear all the grime away.

*MARIA appears. She watches what is happening, takes out a box of
cigarettes and lights up. Throws the cigarette box away.*

*RITA picks up the plastic roll as if tidying up but then does not
know what to do with it; looks at the MAN (her father) as if to
ask – what's this?*

MAN: Rita. Don't –

*The MAN takes the roll from RITA and carefully puts it back in its
place without saying anything. As she turns to go, she accidentally
bumps into him so that he almost loses his balance.*

THE BRIDE/RITA: *(Laughs as she disappears.)*

Come on, Dad… I'm just dreaming…

MARIA: We balance between past and present.

Between forgetting and memory.

Not too much or too little of anything –

You get sick.

Of memories, of what happened,

of silence.

I talked and talked and talked

about everything that happened.

I could have written a book, I used to say.

Then I stopped talking.

Now I can see it in people's bodies.

MARIA also finds herself a seat among the audience, where SOFIA is already sitting. SOFIA suddenly begins talking – first to the person alongside, then to more and more.

SOFIA: I say "I remember",

Then at once I hear: "Forget it."

I say "I don't remember, it's hazy –

Then I hear: "Don't forget."

Now Sofia speaks directly to the MAN and he listens attentively.

When I'm asleep and you wake up to go to work or to make us a coffee and you quietly leave the bedroom:

Please, leave the door open and let me breathe.

Don't leave me behind a closed door –

2. Her Own Happy Life

The MAN/PEDRO picks up the plastic roll and looks once more at the audience. He breaks it open and thin slips of paper covered with tiny writing burst out. He is unable to contain them and they fall towards the floor. Trying to catch them, he loses his balance and falls, full length, on the floor. SOFIA leaps up, anxious for him, and beats a path towards her husband.

SOFIA: *(To the audience, on her way to PEDRO.)* Excuse me, excuse me – sorry.

PEDRO: *(At the same time.)* Fuck!

He struggles to get up and again is about to say something to the audience. What is it that he wants to say? Something about the papers in the roll? Something about what it was like in prison or that he still has sleepless nights sometimes, nights when he can't keep the memories at bay? But he doesn't know how he can say it. SOFIA reaches him and helps him up.

SOFIA: *(To PEDRO.)* You alright? Pedro?

PEDRO pushes her away, irritated.

PEDRO: Yeah, yeah. Don't… I'm alright.

SOFIA: The doctor said you had to be careful.

Your knees are so weak, you risk having to sit in a wheelchair –

PEDRO: I don't want to use a stick.

SOFIA: You have to go careful.

PEDRO: Forget it.

Two girls in the background whisper and giggle together. It's their daughter, RITA, and her new friend, IRENE. They are around fourteen or fifteen and stand closely together, talking quietly.

SOFIA: She said you had to train them up.

PEDRO: I know.

SOFIA: It awakens too many feelings for you. I should've done it.

PEDRO: I wanted to do it –

SOFIA: You need to start using that crutch –

PEDRO: … and I did.

The two girls laugh out loud, carry on whispering, now louder. PEDRO is clearly in pain.

SOFIA: So I saw.

She's coming with her new friend.

Don't let her see that it hurts; don't.

PEDRO: As long as you don't go on about it.

SOFIA: It's embarrassing for her. We agreed, didn't we, that she should live her own life.

PEDRO: Her own <u>happy</u> life. You forgot the happy.

More laughter from the girls, they arrive.

SOFIA: She deserves it.

RITA: We're going swimming.

PEDRO: Good. *(To IRENE.)* Hello.

IRENE: *(Shakes hands with PEDRO, then SOFIA.)* Hi, Irene. Irene.

SOFIA: Hi.

RITA: Where's my swimsuit? It's gone. I've looked for it everywhere.

IRENE: *(Whisper to RITA.)* Ask about what's in the cupboard.

RITA: Shhh.

SOFIA: *(Guarded.)* Have you been in my cupboard?

RITA: *(Lying.)* No.

SOFIA: Rita?

RITA: I haven't.

IRENE supresses her laughter. RITA gives her a murderous look.

RITA: *(Contd.)* I was looking for my swimsuit, wasn't I? And I couldn't find it!

PEDRO: Let her get a new one.

SOFIA: You want to buy a new one?

141

RITA: I wouldn't mind a red one.

IRENE: That'd look lovely out in the blue ocean.

RITA: Wouldn't it? Really nice. *(To her father.)* You got pain in your knee again?

PEDRO: No, no. Just twisted it a bit. It's nothing.

RITA: *(Worried, to SOFIA.)* Mum, what's the matter with his knee?

SOFIA: *(Giving RITA money.)* Nothing. Here.

RITA: *(Very happy and surprised.)* Thanks!

RITA and IRENE go, laughing.

RITA: *(To IRENE, as they leave.)* You know I dreamed I was getting married – and what a wedding dress!

The girls giggle again, clearly thinking what an absurd dream it is.

SOFIA: Born in another world, that's what she is.

Like us. Our relationship. That's where we became us, if you get me?

We should've stayed. It would've been easier.

What we began there should've continued there.

She seems worried… she didn't have a care in the world there.

We fought to have decent lives, so I thought we could live those lives there.

For her sake.

PEDRO: But we promised each other that we'd come home when it was possible, didn't we?

SOFIA: But for her it was home there.

PEDRO glares at her.

PEDRO: This is where we belong and it's here that a job needs doing.

SOFIA: One you're too weak to do.

PEDRO: If we'd stayed, you could of course have missed out on your bad conscience for not doing anything.

SOFIA: So what is it you do? Talk with the old boys, is that enough?

SOFIA picks up the cigarette box that MARIA threw away earlier and starts fiddling with it, carefully and systematically tearing it apart. PEDRO stands watching her, glaring.

3. Interrogation

The three interrogations are very similar but differ rhythmically – each goes faster in turn, as what is illogical becomes clearer and clearer. The participants themselves choose if they wish to tell the truth about themselves or the characters they are playing, but they must begin by answering with their own names. The sequences should feel just as much like personality tests in magazines as serious interrogations with the military/the police. There is great scope for improvisation here. The three actors interrogating each other may by all means address the audience and weave questions and answers together so that all three are simultaneously in action. They may also end the scene by only giving the names and nationalities of fictitious and/or real persons who have disappeared or been killed.

WOMAN 2 is the YOUNG LYDIA. She knits a little teddy bear jersey from a large ball of red wool while watching the interrogations.

WOMAN 3 interrogates MAN

Name: *(Actor's own name.)*

Age: *(Free to choose.)*
Sex: *(The truth.)*
Address: *(An address from the town/city where the piece is being played.)*
Civil status: *(Married/divorced/single.)*
Brothers and sisters: *(Invented names, or none, or deceased.)*
Lover: …That's secret, *(or no answer, or a name.)*
Do you blush: *(Must choose yes or no.)*
Nationality: *(Does not answer.)*
Profession: Actor *(or architect.)*
Favourite colour: *(Free to choose.)*
Passive or active personality: Active.
What kinds of drugs do you use: None.
Do you smoke: *(Yes/no.)*
How many cigarettes a day: *(Tell the truth or lie.)*
Do you work out: A bit.
Do you eat meat: Yes.
Do you eat vegetables: Yes.
Sugar: Yes.
You do know that sugar is bad for you: Yes.
Nationality: *(What the actor feels himself to be.)*
//
Nationality: *(Choose the country/region from where parents/family comes from originally.)*
Nationality: *(Keeps quiet.)*
//
Political party: Political party?
(RAPIDLY) Do you eat fish: Yes.
(RAPIDLY) Political party: None of your business.
/
Member of any organisations? No *(Lies.)*
How often do you work out: Twice a week *(or 3-4).*
Twice? OK. Once. Usually just once. *(Or twice.)*
Political party: None of… no.
Political party: *(Silence.)*
Favourite actor: *(The actor is free to choose.)*

How often do you have a shower? Once a day.
Do you eat salt? Yes.
Political party: ... No –
Political affiliation: *(Does not answer.)*

MAN *interrogates WOMAN 1*

Name: *(Actor's own name.)*
Age: *(Free to choose.)*
Sex: *(The truth.)*
Address: *(An address from the town/city where the piece is being played.)*
Civil status: *(Married/divorced/single.)*
Brothers and sisters: *(Lies or truth.)*
Children: *(Lies or truth.)*
Lover: ... that's secret, *(or no answer, or a name.)*
Do you blush: *(Must answer yes or no.)*
Nationality: *(Does not answer.)*
Profession: Student.
Student. Sure? *(Yes/No/Does not answer.)*
What kinds of drugs do you use: What?
Drugs? None.
Do you smoke: *(Yes/no.)*
How many cigarettes a day: *(The truth or a lie.)*
Do you eat meat: Yes.
Sugar: Yes.
Nationality: *(What the actor feels herself to be.)*
//
Nationality: *(Choose the country/region from where parents/family comes from originally.)*
Nationality: *(Keeps quiet.)*
//
Political party: Political party?
Favourite actor: *(Free to choose.)*
Where were you yesterday? At home.
Favourite colour? *(Free to choose.)*

All day? Yes.
(Rapidly.) Political party: None of your business *(or does not answer.)*
/

Member of any organisations? No *(Lies.)*
How often do you work out: Twice a week *(or 3-4).*
Twice?: OK. Once. Usually just once *(or twice).*
Political party: None of… No.
Political party: *(Silence.)*
How often do you have a shower? Once a day.
Did you have a shower yesterday? Yes.
You do know that salt is bad for you: Yes.
Where were you yesterday? At home.
Address: *(Same as earlier.)*

WOMAN 1 interrogates WOMAN 3

Name: *(Answers own name or the name of one of the other actors.)*
Age: *(Free to choose.)*
Address: *(The same as WOMAN 1 just answered.)*
Civil status: Single.
Lover: … No.
Have you ever been unfaithful: No.
What did you do this morning: What?
This morning: … Went for a jog.
Nationality: *(Does not answer).*
Profession: Journalist.
Favourite colour: *(Free to choose.)*
Favourite food: *(Free to choose.)*
Nationality: *(What the actor feels herself to be.)*
You do know that smoking kills: Yes.
How much do you smoke? Don't smoke at all.
No? *(Does not answer.)*
//
Nationality: *(Choose the country/region from where parents/family comes from originally.)*

Nationality: *(Uncertain, decides to keep quiet.)*
//
Political party: Political party?
Favourite actor: *(Free to choose, lies or truth.)*
Where were you yesterday? At home.
(Rapidly.) Political party: None of your business.
All day? Yes.
//
Member of any organisation: No *(Lies.)*
So you go running: Yes.
How often: Three or four times a week.
Four: Yes… Or sometimes twice maybe…
Where do you go jogging: *(Takes too long.)*
(Rapidly.) Where: Around the neighbourhood.
How often do you have a shower: Once a day.
Political party: *(Silence.)*
Sugar: No.
Salt: Yes.
Political organisation: *(Silence.)*

4. So Little in Comparison

YOUNG LYDIA holds a homemade teddy bear in her hands. The knitting and the large ball of red wool lies beside her.

The couple, ENRIQUE and LYDIA, watch and listen to YOUNG LYDIA as she speaks, as if they are looking back into their past. Perhaps they write down some of what she says on the thin slips of paper.

At length, their daughter, AURORA, starts pulling a long thread from her mother's ball of wool.

YOUNG LYDIA: *(To the audience.)* What was I supposed to say to my daughter? That it was normal for fathers to be in prison?

The other kids' fathers were at home, weren't they, most of them.

At least when they weren't at work.

Or at their mother's, or with brothers, uncles.

So what was I supposed to say to her?

Her first birthday. We were all three together. One, nineteen and twenty years old.

On her second birthday, it was just me and her. I cut out a little paper crown for my princess and had knitted a little teddy bear and filled it with cotton wool. It was red and lovely and soft and she was so happy. She took it to the prison later to show her dad. She sat with it on her lap on the bus going: "Daddy, look!"

AURORA takes the teddy jersey, which has now been finished, and puts it on the teddy bear; shows it to ENRIQUE.

AURORA: Daddy, look!

YOUNG LYDIA: On her third birthday, it was just me and her.

And on her fourth.

By coincidence, her fifth birthday was one of the few days we were allowed to visit her dad in prison, and it was so strict there that I knew, even after the three hours on the bus, it was quite possible we'd have to travel the three hours back again without seeing him – but it was the girl's birthday after all, so that couldn't happen.

But then it did.

Her sixth –

We celebrated her seventh birthday in our new homeland –
//

No, I don't want to think about that at the moment –

YOUNG LYDIA and AURORA meet in the chaos of yarn and try to wind it up again – but this leads to just more chaos. ENRIQUE finds the teddy bear amidst the chaos and gives it to AURORA.

AURORA: Of course I didn't understand what she did; I only thought about him. Who was having such an awful time.

Now I can see that she was a hero too.

(Points at LYDIA.) Here's my hero. The one who kept things going. Who got through everything.

ENRIQUE goes over to LYDIA.

LYDIA: I don't remember anything.

AURORA: Yes, you do, Mum. I know you remember some things –

ENRIQUE reads the tiny slips of paper, then hands them on to LYDIA, but she just screws them up and throws them away without reading them. AURORA picks them up, flattens them out and tries to read them.

LYDIA: But what I remember isn't worth anything. It was so little in comparison with his memories. So powerful, so dreadful. In comparison with the others. I'm here thinking and – no, my memories are not like worth anything – no, Aurora, not in comparison with –

AURORA: *(Speechless.)* What?

LYDIA: It all seems kind of so little.

AURORA: But it was our life.

LYDIA: What?

AURORA: Our life.

LYDIA: Maybe it's that… that… what they remember is so much more. You can see it in them. The pain. Sometimes the fear. Still.

AURORA: So?

LYDIA: What are my memories in comparison?

AURORA: But they're the only thing we have to relate to.

I remember Dad saying –

I can't have been more than about four or five, and Mum and me were visiting him. For half an hour. I remember the smell.

//

He said: "I'm your daddy."

Almost like he was trying to remind himself, I've thought later, because the words kept grinding round and round in my head. Time and again through all these years.

ENRIQUE: "I'm your daddy."

AURORA: Why did he say that?

As if I didn't know he was my dad?

ENRIQUE: Every time you were supposed to come I made you a card and wrote a poem for you that you could take home. They were approved and rubber-stamped by the sensor and then you were allowed to have them.

ENRIQUE reads from one of the tiny sheets. Perhaps AURORA reads too.

"Little daughter, sunbeam of the house, you laugh and laugh. The laughter in your eyes lights up the world.

Laugh so much that the light reaches me."

LYDIA: *(To the audience.)* I waited and waited and waited. Waited for him to die, waited for him to be released, waited for us to go into exile, waited for him to die –

/

Waited for his parents to forgive me, waited to visit him, waited for the bus, for the post, for her to grow up, for him to die or survive, for his father to look at me, for money for food, for work, to put her to bed, to pick her up, to deliver her, at the babysitter's in the evening, in the morning, for the years to pass, for him to be released or die –

Waited for her to get bigger, waited for him to come back to me so that my life could go on.

/

Why should I remember the time that was just waiting and pain, worry and waiting?

5. We're Just Looking After Them

MARIA: *(To the audience.)* I was living in a boarding house in the middle of the city. Had no idea where I was supposed to go; to put it simply, I was on the run. I couldn't be found and it was the same with my friends. And that's how we lost each other. I just hoped to find them, like one day they'd suddenly be right in front of me on the street or in the lounge of the boarding house or I don't know what. I didn't know where anyone was. There were more of us there at the boarding house – in the same situation.

So we were careful about mixing, both among ourselves and with others. Careful about everything.

/

There were two elderly women who rented one of the rooms. They always kept very much to themselves. Were living there with two children around about four or five. The children were so sweet and kind of fearful. Remember the way they looked at you. Great big eyes. I wanted to talk to them, cheer them up a bit. But the women just sent the children into the room and shied away. "They're so sweet," I said, "are they your grandchildren?"

"We're just looking after them", the women said, evasively, and walked off, slipping back into their room. Took in trays of food. Stopped showing themselves altogether.

We're just looking after them... Poor kids.

//

Poor parents.

6. Mum's Cupboard (1)

RITA picks up slips of paper from the floor, also those that fell when PEDRO opened the plastic roll.

While RITA is talking, EVA, at a distance, systematically goes through old yellowed newspapers, throwing them away when she clearly does not find what she is looking for.

WOMAN 1 and the MAN make notes and attend to what RITA is saying.

RITA: *(To the audience.)* I remember when I was little –

I was allowed to go in my mum's cupboard.

Get out old boxes with necklaces and rings

and sunglasses –

I remember –

Remember she said you can go in this box or that box,

but you mustn't touch the one at the bottom, underneath the shoes.

Never.

And I never asked what was in it.

MAN: Why not?

RITA: She was so serious. Maybe that's why.

I remember I wanted to ask my mother about when she was imprisoned.

If she was tortured.

Because she was. I know she was. I felt it.

I think about it. Imagine it. It's almost like I know what it was like.

I have to stop

Thinking like that.

Thinking about it

MAN: Did you ask?

RITA: No. I didn't dare. Was scared of –

That it might set her off thinking.

Make her go strange –

The MAN takes the slips of paper from her, shows them to the audience.

WOMAN 1: I just wanted to borrow a roll of tape, just wanted to get a stapler –

I remember her saying "Not that drawer, you're not to go in there."

But then I was little –

7. We Love Her, Don't We

EVA dries her hands and approaches her husband, HECTOR. The landscape is now a chaos of yarn and yellowed newspapers.

EVA: Hector?

HECTOR shakes his head.

EVA: *(Contd.)* She's behaving more and more strangely.

HECTOR: It's just the way she is.

EVA: We need to tell her.

HECTOR: She's always been like that. A bit awkward.

EVA: You don't know that… We don't know what she was… what she –

HECTOR: She needed someone like us.

EVA: But what if it's hereditary, some kind of sickness, something we don't know anything about –

HECTOR: We got to know everything.

EVA: We? You did!

HECTOR: We love her, don't we –

EVA: Exactly. We must tell her.

HECTOR: What?

EVA: Don't you remember anything? Don't you remember how much she cried? All those hours of crying?

She sat with her knees tucked up under her chin – that tiny little girl, and just cried –

HECTOR: It passed. She's been fine. Just fine.

EVA: Yes. No one could have loved her like we do. Like we've done. Given her what we've given her.

But she's so strange…

HECTOR: She's completely normal.

EVA: You don't know her.

HECTOR: That's enough.

EVA: You weren't there.

HECTOR: Eva –

EVA: You were working all the time –

HECTOR: If it hadn't been for me –

//

With you who couldn't –

I gave you the child you couldn't have.

//

Forget it.

EVA: What did you do to them?

HECTOR: Nothing.

EVA: But you knew something. You were always so strange when you came home. Your face all stiff. Like this.

THE DAUGHTER appears (WOMAN 2). They don't notice her. She looks at them, her face grey.

EVA: *(Contd.)* Like this. Expressionless.

HECTOR: Nothing.

EVA: Without feeling.

HECTOR takes hold of EVA – there's a feeling that he has a great deal of aggression inside him, even though it is not otherwise expressed.

HECTOR: Forget it!

They notice THE DAUGHTER. HECTOR releases EVA and EVA runs over to THE DAUGHTER and hugs her.

EVA: My little girl.

THE DAUGHTER is motionless. Allows herself to be hugged; looks at them with distant, mistrustful eyes.

8. Happy Happy Shopping Family

The three friends, RITA, IRENE and TATIANA, at RITA's house. They are around fourteen years old.

PEDRO, RITA's father is there, but in his own space, not with the girls.

IRENE: Say something then! Rita, say something!

RITA: I don't talk about it to anyone.

TATIANA: About what?

IRENE: *(To TATIANA.)* Never.

TATIANA: About what?

RITA is keen to share her secret but dare not. Her parents do not talk to her about it so she is also quite unsure as to what actually happened to them.

RITA: My mum and dad.

IRENE: *(To TATIANA.)* Before she was born, you know.

TATIANA: You don't talk about it at all? *(To IRENE.)* Doesn't she? *(To RITA.)* You do!

IRENE: No, she doesn't actually.

RITA: *(Dramatically, like wishing to share a secret.)* My mother and father –

IRENE: *(Whispers to TATIANA.)* There was someone who just disappeared –

TATIANA: *(Whispers, to IRENE.)* What? Disappeared?

IRENE: Shh – *(Aloud, to TATIANA, but such that RITA is meant to hear.)* They were in prison.

RITA: They got so thin.

IRENE: Oh come on! They were tortured. You said so!

RITA: Stop.

TATIANA: *(To IRENE.)* Yeah, stop.

RITA: *(To IRENE.)* So shut up then!

TATIANA: *(To RITA.)* Do you think it's gross?

IRENE: *(To TATIANA.)* They nearly died too. It's you that's bugging her!

TATIANA: Me?

RITA: *(To IRENE.)* It's actually you right now.

IRENE: *(To TATIANA.)* It was you who said it was horrible. OK, who cares? *(To RITA.)* Shall we go in the cupboard in your parents' bedroom?

RITA: Are you crazy, or what!?

IRENE: You're such a pain. So tell her then!

RITA: What?

IRENE: How you weren't born here and stuff. That they got to know each other abroad and that you were born there and lived there. Tell her about everything, about what they did before.

RITA: *(Seriously trying to tell them both something.)* It's quite…

IRENE: *(Interrupts, to TATIANA.) Her parents were in prison, really. (To RITA.)*: Poor you.

TATIANA: So what had they done? Killed somebody? *(Laughs.)*

RITA: *(Superior.)* They fought for higher wages and stuff.

IRENE: You can't change the world from inside a prison!

RITA: Yes, you can.

IRENE: "Yes, you can." What do you know about it?

You said your father never told you anything about it!

TATIANA: Hasn't he?

RITA: It's not so easy to talk about, if you've been through such things.

IRENE: "Such things"?

TATIANA: *(To RITA.)* What about your mother?

IRENE: *(To TATIANA.)* I don't suppose your mum and dad have ever been in prison, have they?

TATIANA: Of course not.

IRENE: *(To RITA.)* So say something then!

TATIANA: *(To RITA.)* Tell us!

IRENE and TATIANA threaten RITA so that she backs off and they all move closer to PEDRO. RITA backs off further and trips over the mess on the floor, gets up again, continues to back off – closer and closer to PEDRO who follows what's going on, ominously calm.

PEDRO: What's going on?

RITA: Nothing.

PEDRO: Is there someone here?

RITA: *(Pushing PEDRO away.)* Just a couple of friends, Dad. Don't come in. Don't say anything. Don't –

RITA turns back towards the girls, pretending nothing has happened, gets them to move away from PEDRO.

TATIANA: What was that?

RITA: Nothing.

PEDRO looks at them, quietly, slightly scarily. He begins walking back and forth, on guard, yet restlessly.

IRENE: *(Playing, to RITA and TATIANA.)* This is the past.

TATIANA: *(Inventing, with conviction, to RITA.)* Just like you are your mother.

IRENE: They're going to hassle you.

TATIANA: Force you to talk.

IRENE: You have to keep your mouth shut.

TATIANA: And smile!

RITA: Don't shake. Don't smile. Just say nothing.

PEDRO: *(Calling out, while walking back and forth further away.)* What are you doing?

RITA: Nothing.

IRENE: Don't smile. Just stay silent.

RITA: Don't shake. Keep calm.

IRENE: Stay cool!

They laugh with bravado and madness.

RITA: Yes! Stay cool and keep your mouth shut.

TATIANA: Like you're not even bothered.

IRENE: *(To TATIANA.)* Grab her.

The two girls grab hold of RITA as if they were her jailors. TATIANA giggles.

IRENE: Talk! Name? Address?

TATIANA: Do you like sugar?

IRENE: Cell phone number?

RITA says nothing. They press her down onto her knees, twist her arms behind her back, roughly, brutally. IRENE asks TATIANA to take pictures with her cell phone. Selfies with the victim. They laugh, shrilly singing a nursery rhyme while they harass her and repeatedly shrieking: Name, address, cell phone number and other questions that we recognise from the interrogations earlier. But RITA does not answer. IRENE tells TATIANA to force RITA's mouth open. RITA screams out something incomprehensible; it no longer seems like play and, taken aback, they let go of her all at once. She collapses. They try to get her to her feet, but she is unresponsive.

PEDRO: What's going on?

IRENE: *(Innocently.)* Nothing. *(To TATIANA, whispers.)* What's the matter with her? Jesus. Should we tell her father?

TATIANA: *(Whispers.)* No way.

RITA sits up.

IRENE: Rita! Hello – what was all that about? Scared we were going to torture you for real or something?

RITA: Just pack it in, Irene, you don't know anything.

RITA shakes herself and pulls herself together. IRENE and TATIANA are scared. RITA is ready for a new round.

RITA: Shall we start again?

IRENE and TATIANA nod hesitantly.

RITA: *(Contd.)* I'll start. I remember that…

IRENE: About what's in the cupboard!

RITA: *(Deliberately not listening.)* I went to the shopping centre today; wanted to buy a new swimsuit. A red swimsuit for the blue ocean. My idea was to –

IRENE: *(To TATIANA.)* It was my idea.

RITA: *(Looks at IRENE – triumphantly.)* To leave everything and just swim.

IRENE: Blue sea, blue sky. Red swimsuit. The perfect combination.

TATIANA: Leave everything?

RITA: *(Wanting to scare.)* Everything for ever. A red stripe of blood was to trail behind me as I swam, weaker and weaker, in the endless deep blue ocean. The big shining knife sank slowly down into the depths below me and in the end I had no strength left, my life was ebbing out and I couldn't keep on the surface any more…

IRENE: So why aren't you dead now then?

TATIANA: Where's your swimsuit?

IRENE: You didn't even buy it!

RITA: No. I knew the building. I walked up towards it; of course the plan was to go in. I thought I'd play the role of a customer… but then I didn't know the language.

TATIANA: *(Inventing.)* So you tried Chinese!

RITA: No, stupid. I couldn't communicate with anyone whatsoever. They talked completely weirdly.

TATIANA: What? In the shopping centre?

IRENE: You mean you don't know? She wasn't able to just be a customer there, at that place, don't you see?

RITA: *(Precocious.)* I became an outsider, one who doesn't understand the geography or the language.

TATIANA: The language?

RITA: The shopping centre language.

IRENE: Come on! Don't you know anything? Her father was <u>there</u>.

TATIANA: Shopping?

IRENE: It hasn't always been a shopping centre, if you get me. It used to be a prison, imagine. Doesn't anybody know that? Seriously?

Kind of "happy happy shopping family" – I guess that's what they want. These days.

TATIANA: *(Doubtful.)* It doesn't say anywhere that it was a prison there before. You sure?

IRENE: Dead sure! *(Laughs.)* Like there'd be a sign: "Now then, son, would you like an ice cream and some new toys or shall we read about how there used to be a prison here?"

RITA: Who sat in the cell where they now sell ice cream?

TATIANA: So was that where he was?

RITA: He went out to buy some cigs and they grabbed him. Someone he'd been working with had been tortured into saying his name. Snitched.

TATIANA: *(Doesn't understand the word.)* Snitched?

IRENE: Out to buy cigs; shame.

9. A Part of the World Only I Have Been in (1)

One of the others brings on a walking stick for PEDRO – he doesn't want it but, after a bit, starts using it anyway.

PEDRO: *(To the audience.)* Nobody asks.

It's so big, like a world of its own –

A part of the world only I have been in,

A dark continent

Where nobody's going and that nobody's interested in.

All that, they say, or think, or at least I think they do,

All that dreadful business –

Is over now. It needs to be forgotten.

But there's so much more to it.

Stories, friendships, secrets, fears –

Life was so vivid, and different, and –

All the things we managed to do despite

Despite –

Everything. Our strength.

//

Yes, I walk a bit funny. I don't see well and I run rather strangely –

But do you know why?

Do you want to hear why?

Then I get angry or feel provoked.

And then it's best not to say anything.

10. Stripped of Humanity

MARIA: I was caught.

I knew I wasn't supposed to shake.

Down the corridors.

One door up and another. One more.

Down the corridors.

They wanted to scare me. And they did.

They managed that, for life.

We were walking past. A door opened,

just by chance –

The hinges squeaked, at least enough to get me to turn round,

enough for all my attention to be trained on a door swinging wide open at that very moment.

And that's where they were hanging. Loads of women.

Hanging up –

Their arms tied above their heads and hung up. Like this.

ONE OF THE OTHERS: Like this?

All lift their arms above their heads as if hanging by their hands and elbows.

MARIA: Yes. Like that. I don't think they were moving.
I didn't hear any sounds either. Maybe because I was in shock, I don't know. *(She shivers.)*

They led me on. Down the corridor.

That light green colour *(Shudders.)*

Pretended like they didn't know I'd seen.

Like it wasn't a threat.

The naked bodies hanging there,

Like they were animals.

Carcasses.

Stripped of humanity.

ONE OF THE OTHERS: Completely naked?

MARIA: Just a blindfold over their eyes.

"Anything wrong, miss? We just want to ask you a few questions, miss."

They opened another door. Told me to go in, sit down.

I did. I wasn't shaking.

/

And I was allowed to go.

That time I was allowed to go. Well I didn't know anything. Didn't have anything to tell them.

Nothing.

11. A Part of the World Only I Have Been in (2)

PEDRO stands upright with his crutch. Sometimes it appears that his legs will give way, but he carries on.

PEDRO: It's like I've lived multiple lives,

been on many journeys.

Even those who mean well, even they

don't want to know,

that we know something they don't, that our experiences make us –

Would it've been better if we'd died?

We survived hell.

"Tell us about hell!"

Yeah, so maybe we did then.

But it became too much; I started censoring myself,

more on each occasion.

Because it's embarrassing.

What my body's gone through is uncomfortable for others.

Can that be possible?

And then I feel a kind of shame too –

Because I don't say anything,

because I *don't* tell them everything.

As if I should, simply to honour those that are gone –

Yes, they raped me.

Yes, they had me crawl around in shit and piss.

Yes, I lay there while they wrapped a rope around my testicles

and pulled me to my feet with it –

Yes, I was blindfolded, had a hood over my head

so they could forget I was human.

So I couldn't see who was carrying out those inhuman acts.

Yes, I got a picana electrica in my butt too and –

Yes, it was my body.

//

And afterwards I washed it with soap,

let it dry in the wind, bathed it in the sea,

climbed the highest mountains –

And looked out over the land,

let the world embrace me again –

12. Tramp, Stop, Listen

YOUNG LYDIA, knitting a child's jersey, identical to the one that the teddy bear is now wearing. AURORA goes over to the young mother and takes the teddy, hugs it. YOUNG LYDIA strokes her head, caresses her hair, continues knitting.

AURORA: *(To the audience.)* Mummy's hand was… it held me so tightly –

She lifted me up and hugged me against her.

And her heart was hammering away,

and she was wet with sweat,

and… shaking.

And I saw… *(Searches for more – as she wants to remember – but cannot find anything.).*

The mother keeps knitting. AURORA takes the jersey off the teddy, then puts it back on again. Wanting to remember.

LYDIA and ENRIQUE appear together; they listen to her as if looking back.

AURORA: *(Contd.)* The first thing I remember… is church.

Me and my aunt there.

The church and the military are kind of linked.

Everything is secret.

"Don't tell Mummy that I take you to church"

Don't tell the others that daddy is in prison.

Don't talk,

don't remember,

don't make any noise.

In church with my aunt breathing calmly and quietly,

there was a kind of sigh throughout the enormous space.

And everyone moving with short steps, making a shy little cross in front of them.

And I –

I remember… the smell of sweat and shoes and earth and the shadows –

And Mummy's hand,

and Daddy who had such thin fingers.

What did he eat actually,

what did they give him to eat?

Smile and be quiet, said my aunt.

Don't say anything –

Nothing.

Looks at YOUNG LYDIA knitting, talks directly to her:

AURORA: *(Contd.)* I don't remember that smile.

The young mother smiles at AURORA. Then AURORA sees LYDIA and ENRIQUE, her parents as they are now. LYDIA puts things to rights, making things pleasant. But AURORA is not part of her parents' togetherness; she is only an observer. ENRIQUE strokes LYDIA's head, caresses her hair.

ENRIQUE: *(To the audience and the others.)* It was a warm autumn day – it must have been latish in the afternoon because it was quite late when they came after us.
I met a friend out on the street, he said now you need to

get away. They know who you are. But what about my
family –

I can't, I have to fetch them, I've got a little daughter.

A little daughter.

And I went home.

*LYDIA covers everything spread out over the floor with an enormous
table cloth.*

ENRIQUE: *(Contd.)* And – I remember… the smell of burnt
people, I remember…

LYDIA: Forget it. Stop –

We're about to eat. Here – I've made your favourite -

You have to enjoy everything that's good. It's over.

ENRIQUE: And then they came to get us, and we'd just
managed to hide every trace. Put everything needing to
be hidden in recesses in the floor, wrapped blankets and
clothes round documents and weapons, then floorboards
over the top. So you couldn't hear it when you walked
across the floor. That anything was out of the ordinary.
We'd gone back and forth across the floor, tramping,
stopping, checking the sound:

*He tramps on the large cloth that LYDIA has spread out. Tramps,
stops and listens.*

*While he does so, she tries to clear everything under the large cloth. At
length, she starts tramping too. Perhaps the two others also join in.*

ENRIQUE: *(Contd.)* Does that sound normal? Is there any
chance whatever that doesn't sound right?

Tramp, stop, listen.

Tramp, stop, listen.

Tramp, stop, listen.

And then they come storming in – and what does she do?
Our one-year-old who'd just learnt to walk.

Tramp, stop, listen –

Tramp, stop, listen –

He laughs. LYDIA too, softly.

ENRIQUE: *(Contd.)* And that's how we got caught.

LYDIA: All three of us.

/

She doesn't smile in any of her childhood pictures, did
you know that?

They look at each other for a long time.

ENRIQUE: You supported me.

LYDIA: I did. I still do. And now we must eat.

*He embraces her. LYDIA following, he leads her in a kind of dance
in the silence; he almost loses his balance but she supports him.
They chuckle mildly.*

YOUNG LYDIA finishes off the child's jersey – gives it to AURORA.

AURORA: *(To the audience.)* I remember wearing this! I can feel
myself on the inside of this little jumper.

(To the teddy bear.) And I had you under my arm!

*YOUNG LYDIA laughs – LYDIA and ENRIQUE come closer, they
too smiling.*

AURORA: *(Contd.)* I must've taken little kiddy-steps, but in my
memory we like strode off, teddy and me, to go and find
Daddy, to tell him that he had to come home.

Mummy must have been terrified when she came running
after us and found us down the road.

LYDIA: Terrified.

AURORA: Imagine I can remember what wearing this jumper was like!

YOUNG LYDIA goes off. AURORA looks helplessly at her parents.

ENRIQUE: She was so little.

LYDIA: So very, very little.

13. Mum's Cupboard (2)

The actors tramp about the cloth, noticing everything that is lying underneath it.

RITA: *(With the paper slips in her hands.)* I just wanted to borrow a roll of tape, just wanted to get a stapler –

I remember her saying: "Not that drawer, you're not to go in there."

SOFIA: *(In the situation.)* What are you doing? Hands off – you know you're not allowed!

RITA: But that was before – Mum, I'm big now.

What's the problem?

SOFIA: *(Cautiously.)* It belongs to an exhibition.

RITA: Why haven't you spoken about it?

SOFIA: It was for your sake, my lovely, for your sake –

She is unable to force herself to say more – SOFIA and RITA look at each other for a long time. Everything is silent.

RITA: *(To the audience.)* Anything but that silence, anything but that.

I grew up with it, the fear of asking, the fear of knowing –

The fear of everything that is there – and that I know nothing about.

Because it is there, isn't it?

Mum!?

The MAN shows a few of the small slips of paper.

MAN: Look what I've found! Look at these tiny sheets –

I found them in my father's desk.

I just wanted to borrow a roll of tape, just wanted to get a stapler.

I remember him saying –

WOMAN 3: Not that drawer,

You're not to go in there.

But that was when I was little.

Not now.

MAN: He said it should be put on exhibition.

Tell me, I said.

SOFIA: *(With the densely covered slips of paper.)* A back bent over the thinnest of sheets,

The tiny letters, in the toilet, by the light from one of the apertures high above –

One standing guard, one writing –

RITA: But why are they here? In the bedroom?

RITA, MAN and WOMAN 3 show the slips to the audience, beginning to hand them out.

RITA: *(To each, as she goes, contd.)* Look, careful, see how thin they are – look how tiny the letters are – look!

MAN: *(Ad lib.)* Look – pass it on, pass it on –

WOMAN 3: *(Ad lib.)* Look at this – shall we just throw them away?

RITA: *(Ad lib.)* Look here – pass it on –

SOFIA: Careful!

RITA: *(Indicating one of the audience.)* Now he can have a look, pass it on! And you – pass it on!

Shall we throw them?

MAN: Hide them?

RITA: What shall we do?

WOMAN 3: They were in a box in her cupboard, and I was little, didn't understand anything. You can borrow what you like of my necklaces and old sunglasses, she said.

SOFIA: Just *don't* go in that box. Never even touch it.

MAN: But now I did just the same, because that box can't stay inside the cupboard inside the bedroom anymore –

RITA: They were in the box in her cupboard. Soon they'll be mine. What am I supposed to do with them?

The sheets are sent around amongst the audience. SOFIA looks worried.

SOFIA: *(Wanting to get them back, talks to individuals in the audience.)* Careful! Can you give me that back?

Takes a slip from an audience member.

RITA: *(To SOFIA.)* So read it out then!

SOFIA: *(To the audience.)* Why should I be forced to talk about it?

(Irritated, to RITA.): What am I even doing up here on stage?

RITA: *(To SOFIA.)* This is life, Mum. This is your scene.

There's nothing you can do about it.

Here I am. Here you are.

14. Her Heart Said Stop

SOFIA reads the sheet she has in her hand, gives it to RITA. RITA reads it and looks up to see HECTOR getting out his military coat from under the large cloth. SOFIA gathers the sheets she herself has written during the previous scenes.

RITA: *(Reading aloud.)* I remember I was always afraid, always.

HECTOR puts his coat on. RITA gives the sheet to HECTOR. He reads it quickly then throws it away. The others become part of the audience.

HECTOR: I remember I was always afraid, always.

That I put my uniform on and knew that if I didn't get them, then they would get me. It's 'war', the top brass said, a war we have to win. Those of us who know better. These people are crazy: kids with twisted ideals of freedom who want to destroy society, destroy everything for us; people who have no idea about the realities of life; fantasists who think we can share money that doesn't exist.

/

Now you're not a weak little shit, are you?

Show us you can make it clear that we're not tolerating it. Can you do that?

Can you do it or are you too weak?

I wasn't weak. Not afraid.

Never afraid. That's for kids.

//

Now I'm someone completely different. I've put a thick, black line through the whole period.

It got so one-dimensional.

"I'm going to kill myself."

Time after time after time.

She was the one who wanted to have children. I did her a good turn. She couldn't manage anything.

Women – so irresolute. First she wants to and then she doesn't.

/

And then our little princess arrived and she just had to get on with it. That was what was best for everyone.

But she couldn't manage to live with the secret; it just got worse and worse.

It was probably the best way out for her. Quick. She managed that alright.

Pills. No one could understand it.

It was her heart that said stop.

Suddenly THE DAUGHTER is there. She looks at him, says nothing. He doesn't notice her.

(Cries.) I've lost her. I've lost her. I've lost her.

He looks up, sees THE DAUGHTER.

And our daughter…

THE DAUGHTER looks at him a long time before turning and walking away – he stands and watches her go.

15. Moonlight

HECTOR is like a kind of silhouette, still wearing his military coat.

MARIA: A soldier in silhouette as they blow our door open.

The full moon shines into the room through the door,
right behind the soldier,

Lighting up the room so it's blue and cold. He stands there
with his machine gun aiming at me,

And I sit up in our bed in the lounge –

Rub my eyes, and only when I get up does the fear hit me
in the stomach.

Barefoot on the floor bathing in ice-cold moonlight.

And the soldiers tramp in: pushing, shoving, toppling
things over –

Hitting –

And searching and searching and searching,

And I put on my vest, trousers and shoes,

Telling them they must be quiet:

The neighbours' kids are asleep –

But no –

//

Later – a hatch high up in the wall of the dark cell

Was the only light.

I looked out, looked out and saw –

A moon –

For days and nights I looked up at that hatch.

And I imagined him who'd stood there with his machine
gun,

a silhouette in the moonlight –

It stuck in my mind's eye and my gaze never left that little
hatch of light.

They had me sit a long time in that cell. A long time.

It did for my eyes.

//

And when I saw him standing there in the doorway with the moon behind him, I thought about all the women I'd seen through the door the first time they took me in, and I knew that now it was serious.

Now it was my turn.

Shoot me now, I thought; don't let me reach prison alive.

Not that –

Not me –

16. My Story

SOFIA rolls together a number of the tiny slips of paper she has collected and ties a fine silk ribbon around the roll.

RITA and IRENE appear; they are around nineteen years old. SOFIA doesn't see them immediately.

PEDRO is also present, but at a little distance.

RITA: Of course I was born there and it was a totally different country, a different world. It was just like we were in two totally different worlds.

IRENE: But didn't they get to know each other there?

RITA: That didn't help. They both came from here, didn't they?

IRENE: Didn't they talk to you?

RITA: Yes, of course. But they only talked about, like, normal things. Like – "What do you want for breakfast?", "Shall we go down to the swimming pool?" Stuff like that.

IRENE: "We love you"?

RITA: They managed that much.

IRENE: Maybe they didn't want to say anything because you were too little to understand?

RITA: I guess.

IRENE: Because you can't really talk to a child about things like that.

RITA: You can soon get too big too. And, like, not care anymore. You've got enough with yourself.

IRENE: Haven't they told you anything about how they were tortured?

RITA notices SOFIA.

RITA: Shhh.

RITA gesticulates to IRENE to keep her mouth shut. Mimes cutting her own throat etc. SOFIA approaches, carrying the roll of papers tied with silk ribbon.

SOFIA: So this is my scene, is it?

RITA: Yes. Well – right now it's more like mine, or ours. *(Indicating IRENE.)*

SOFIA: *(Wanting to leave.)* OK.

RITA: Mum. Stop. Come.

SOFIA turns around, still holding the roll of papers.

It's your scene. Go on.

IRENE: Go on.

//

SOFIA: *(To RITA.)* We're the same age. You and me. Nineteen.

IRENE snickers. SOFIA has already entered her story; is perhaps slightly 'strange'.

RITA: *(Laughs, correcting her mother.)* Irene and me are nineteen!

SOFIA: Nineteen! And I have to leave where I'm living with my boyfriend as fast as I can.

RITA: With Dad, or…?

SOFIA: Someone else.

We've got to go because we've found out that they're after us. I'd only been to a couple of meetings. And he – hadn't done anything.

PEDRO sighs.

RITA: What kind of meetings?

SOFIA: Er… About better wages, working hours. Strikes. Fairness. And then… then they were after us. After me. I needed a place to hide so I went back to my parents and asked if I could live at home for a while.

IRENE becomes part of the audience. PEDRO moves a little closer.

SOFIA: *(Contd.)* "Please, Mum!"

I was standing on the steps and Mum was standing in the doorway:

"No", she said.

"Please let me in!"

"NO"

"NO"

"NO"

Mum was scared, and Dad was standing behind her, scared and spineless:

"NO"

"NO"

"NO"

179

And I turned round,

And I walked down the steps

And I cried

And I dried my tears

And I needed to

And I got help from a kind man in the organisation, someone who understood that I had to have a place to live, to be looked after.

SOFIA stops. She glances down at the roll with the ribbon round it that she has been holding all the while – gives it to RITA.

PEDRO comes closer; he has his walking stick with him but doesn't lean on it.

RITA: Dad, you say something too. *(Including the audience.).*
Tell us something.

PEDRO: Not now.

RITA: Go on, about what happened when we moved back.
That story.

PEDRO doesn't wish to talk.

RITA: *(Contd., to IRENE and the audience.)* One day, in the street, he said hello to someone he thought looked really familiar.
"Hello",

How are you doing, he thought even, like friendly.

And then he suddenly realised –

RITA begins to back away, her eyes wide with fear.

RITA: *(Contd.)* Recognition, terror –

RITA backs away, she loses her balance on the uneven surface and IRENE runs over and grabs her, tries to keep her on her feet.

180

IRENE: What was it he recognised?

RITA tears herself loose, stands upright – in front of PEDRO, her father. She is defiant, wanting to tell more, although she knows that saying this now is upsetting him.

RITA: A man from the past. His torturer.

IRENE: No way!

PEDRO: *(Pushing IRENE away.)* What are you telling her this for?

RITA: She's my friend.

PEDRO: It's my story.

RITA: That's where you're wrong.

PEDRO: How dare you!?

SOFIA runs over, wanting to help RITA as she believes PEDRO might hit her. Stands between them.

RITA: It's not just yours.

PEDRO: *(To the audience and the others.)* What does she know about my hell?

SOFIA: Pedro! Calm down! Pedro!

RITA and PEDRO go each their own way. RITA undoes the silk ribbon around the slips of paper and lays them out in front of the audience. Gives a couple of them to some of those watching.

17. Waiting Time

AURORA appears. LYDIA helps her put on a jersey that is identical to the child-sized one that YOUNG LYDIA knitted. This jersey fits her. It is as if AURORA has become small again.

LYDIA: *(While dressing AURORA.)* Waited to put her to bed, waited to pick her up, waited to deliver her, waited for the childminder, waited in the evening, waited in the morning, waited for the years to pass, waited for him to be released or die, waited for her to get bigger, waited for him to come back to me so that my life could go on.

LYDIA picks up the teddy bear and gives it to YOUNG LYDIA so that she can give it to her DAUGHTER. ENRIQUE and YOUNG LYDIA approach, perhaps one from either side.

YOUNG LYDIA: Waited to go to bed, to get up, to visit him, to be allowed to love him.

She gives the teddy to AURORA and strokes her hair.

Look, here's a card from Daddy: "Sending you a big kiss and a bigger hug. And, if you can disturb Mummy a minute, give her a kiss and a hug and tell her I miss her lots."

AURORA: … so give her a kiss and a hug and tell her I miss her lots.

YOUNG LYDIA: *(To ENRIQUE.)* I miss you.

AURORA: Waited for Mummy to stop waiting.

AURORA has found the little child's jersey. She takes off the large child's jersey and the jersey off the teddy and lays all three alongside one another, ritually. The times meet. Looks at both her mothers.

Mummy was young, pretty, happy –

LYDIA: *(Happily.)* Now I only wait for him to be finished with the paper or to come home from a meeting.

YOUNG LYDIA laughs happily.

AURORA: She had a sweetheart and a baby –

But Daddy was away all the time, at work and at meetings –

Important meetings.

YOUNG LYDIA: But he always came home.

AURORA: Mummy was home with the baby waiting for Daddy.

For him to come home in the evenings.

YOUNG LYDIA: He loved us.

AURORA: He loved me. I know he did. He sang for me.

ENRIQUE hums a lullaby. Takes YOUNG LYDIA's hand. The song unnoticeably transforms into a love song.

Tucked my quilt in around me –

YOUNG LYDIA: He was so big and so gentle –

ENRIQUE and YOUNG LYDIA hold each other.

LYDIA: He loved me. Us.

His hands stroked your head –

YOUNG LYDIA: Played with your hair, with my hair –

LYDIA: His wise eyes, always so kind.

AURORA: But then…

Then she was unlucky – because then he was really gone.

ENRIQUE suddenly stops singing.

LYDIA: A very, very long time.

YOUNG LYDIA wriggles out of ENRIQUE's embrace and puts LYDIA there in her place. YOUNG LYDIA leaves.

AURORA: "But we'll not say any more about that now, will we?" That's what you used to say, always. "Now everything's alright again, sweetie. Time to get up, time to go to bed, time to have breakfast."

AURORA: *(Contd.)* Sometimes you'd be talking in low voices, then stop when I came in. Of course I understood that things weren't always that good for you. Afterwards. But I never got to know anything. Nothing!

ENRIQUE: Why didn't you just ask?

AURORA: What?

ENRIQUE: Why don't you just ask?

AURORA: Because… I'm scared it'll be too… unmanageable.

ENRIQUE: But now I want to tell you. Ask.

AURORA: I'm scared you want to tell me ordinary stuff like population counts, generals and presidents, about US involvement and geography and demography and wages and strikes –

ENRIQUE: Just ask me whatever you like.

AURORA: But what I want to know, Dad, is what it was like for you, what you felt, what happened, what happened to your friends, to Mum. All the things that get you to break down –

That's what I wonder about. Everything that'll make me understand who you have been for me in my life. Who you can and can't be for me. What's my family history?

Why am I the person I am? Is that something you can tell me?

LYDIA: Aurora…

ENRIQUE: *(Not understanding.)* Why you are who you are?

AURORA: *(Fervent.)* Dad, do you think life is just about politics? Or social involvement? Do you?

ENRIQUE: No.

AURORA: It's about us. And about Mum.

ENRIQUE: What are you accusing me of, actually?

AURORA: I can't spend my whole life feeling sorry for you!

ENRIQUE: Sorry for me?

AURORA: Or being scared to say something wrong, then.

ENRIQUE: If you only knew what I'd experienced by the time I was your age –

AURORA: I understand that.

ENRIQUE: *(Fervent, very much like AURORA.)* You're just worried about having enough money to buy yourself a new pair of high-heeled shoes!

AURORA: Shoes! Dad…

ENRIQUE: Go down to the shopping centre, then, to consumer prison –

LYDIA: *(To ENRIQUE.)* Easy.

ENRIQUE: *(To AURORA.)* Let yourself be imprisoned in that hell. Go on!

AURORA: That's not what we're discussing.

LYDIA: We're not going to start discussing anything.

AURORA: Exactly! Nothing. Don't talk about it. Like it's something to be ashamed of!

That's just the way it's always been – you've never changed one bit, Mum!

AURORA leaves.

ENRIQUE: Aurora!

ENRIQUE wants to go after her but LYDIA stops him.

LYDIA: She can't help being young,

ENRIQUE: No –

LYDIA: And she's not personally responsible for capitalism, now is she?

ENRIQUE: No –

LYDIA takes ENRIQUE's hand – lifts it to her cheek.

LYDIA: Or for the time she's born into.

ENRIQUE: No, she isn't either.

LYDIA: You want her to become an activist?

ENRIQUE: Don't you?

LYDIA: I want her to have a good life. If she doesn't have a good life, what's your effort been worth?

ENRIQUE: So what is a good life?

LYDIA: *(Kisses ENRIQUE.)* This is.

ENRIQUE kisses LYDIA. They kiss each other.

18. Time Without Books

ENRIQUE: *(To the audience.)* So many words, so many pages of details, information, secrets –

I'd heard lectures, argued and made notes –

We'd made overviews, registers, tables and forms –

But then they came to get me.

//

At first, we were allowed books.

My cell was like a library.

Some of the books were what they were, others were given new clothes to wear.

We cut out the original pages and glued forbidden texts in behind innocent facades…

//

And then came the time without books –

When everything we read was swept away, when all attempts at communication were censored down to the tiniest of details. How do you survive then?

/

Aurora, are you there?

LYDIA: She can hear you alright.

ENRIQUE: So I wrote down everything I could.

Formulas, dates from history books, lectures on philosophy and anthropology that I remembered.

What had happened and what was happening.

Everything we remembered was noted on these tiny sheets – in miniature handwriting.

We shared it with the others – we smuggled it out, and in to other comrades in other jails –

We wrote down everything we thought someone should get to know.

Writing became important in terms of having existed.

And we had to hide what we wrote,

wherever necessary –

(Laughs.) I had to play the psychologist to get the others to understand you're no less of a man if you have a roll of plastic up your butt…

AURORA approaches, listening attentively to ENRIQUE.

(Serious again.) Writing it down became a way of getting existence to hang together.

And now I can remember the paper, the situation, me writing –

What I was sitting on, where I was –

I remember that I remembered.

//

I remember that I was me.

I remember I was sad, without being sad.

Or that I was happy, without being happy right in this moment.

Or angry. Or beside myself with grief.

It all lives on in me.

But all the same –

That that man was me is totally incomprehensible.

He was a completely different person.

ENRIQUE leaves.

19. The Bride

RITA enters, in the wedding dress. It now looks used – no longer gleaming white.

She picks out a little red yarn at one place, a few old newspapers somewhere else, tiny sheets of paper, a roll of plastic, the military coat. At first, she finds the things sticking out from under the large cloth, then afterwards lifts the cloth to find things underneath. It looks like she is wandering around on an abandoned battlefield.

RITA: *(To the audience, whilst finding things.)* Save it or throw it?

Well, I can't keep it at home. Not now.

Not in my life now.

It's quite simple: I need to create the space for a new life –

A happy one.

I want to clear all the grime away,

(Laughs.) Can't be dealing with all that grief –

RITA energetically tidies away before stopping and speaking to the audience.

(To the audience.) Well, I'm married, aren't I?

Going to have kids.

I'm thinking a big family –

One long table with laughter and noise.

"Pass me the butter",

"You heard what the neighbour's done?",

"Have you done your homework?",

"Want to go to the beach?",

"That tastes fantastic!",

"Can you teach me how to bake?"

All that kind of stuff.

I want my answers to be yes.

"Can I come in?"

"YES!"

(Concerning everything around her on the floor.)
And remember all this at the same time?

RITA picks out a few of the yellowed newspapers, quickly leafs through one or two, as if she thinks she might find something there.

SOFIA appears in the background, she too picks up an old newspaper and leafs through it, throws it aside and takes up another, which she scans carefully, as if she is looking for something in particular. RITA notices her.

Perhaps they were so concerned about being normal, they forgot what life was all about?

SOFIA finds what she is looking for – becomes absorbed in an article and a picture on one of the pages in the newspaper. RITA takes in her mother, the picture of her mother, before speaking to the audience again.

Would I have done the same as Mum and Dad? Would I have dared?

I'm afraid I'm too much of a coward.

SOFIA: You don't choose, it just happens.

It has to happen, otherwise you can't hold out.

RITA: But –

SOFIA: Don't think about it –

Live the life you can live.

RITA: Like the one you didn't get?

Must I, to pay the debt of your pain?

SOFIA lowers the newspaper she has been reading. PEDRO appears, with his walking stick. The three look at each other.

20. He Did Exist, I Can Guarantee It

PEDRO: *(Heavily, almost threateningly.)* It smells stuffy in here.

SOFIA: We can air it out then. Open the door.

PEDRO suddenly takes the newspaper out of her hands; looks at the picture.

What're you doing?

PEDRO: Who's this?

SOFIA takes the newspaper.

SOFIA: Just someone I knew once.

RITA: Who?

PEDRO: Is it him?

RITA: The one that disappeared?

PEDRO: *(Realises his daughter has got to know about 'the one that disappeared'.)* The one that disappeared?

SOFIA: Soon, maybe it'll only be me that remembers him.

The photo's reminiscent of him of course, but it's, like, not him. It's something else that is him.

SOFIA looks at the picture in the newspaper. PEDRO sighs.

SOFIA: *(Contd.)* He exists, doesn't he, if I remember him.

Remember how we got to know each other.

What we talked about, how what… what was special grew up between us.

SOFIA shows RITA the picture of a young man in the old newspaper.

I remember him as quite shy at first. He was leaning against a tree, smoking. Wanting to look careless. I remember thinking how balanced he was, a calm person. Someone who managed to be an observer.

He wasn't calm though, I soon found that out. His restlessness was nothing to do with being nervous, it was impatience. But there he was, standing there observing, calmly and carelessly. He didn't know a soul –

So I gave him a nod, thought that he could at least see a friendly face if nothing else. A face not just concerned with itself. A friendly person, I thought, that could be me. I can play that role here, now – in relation to him.

So I did, and we were soon sitting at a table, quietly talking, sounding out the terrain really, politely skirting the whole issue, and calmly finding out the other's likes and dislikes.

I gradually got to understand how passionate he was, how he dared to ask the most unimaginable questions to get to the bottom of a problem, and it was only then he'd form his opinion. But only when he allowed himself to get physically involved in what he was saying did you get to see the real "him".

That's what I fell in love with.

He did exist. I can guarantee it.

RITA: What happened? How did he disappear?

SOFIA: They were looking for me and couldn't find me. So they took him, I found out later. So that I'd miss him and come looking. And then they'd be able to get hold of me. There was no reason for taking him!

But I'd gone into hiding and never got to know anything about it. No one said anything. Nothing.

RITA holds her mother, comforts her, as if she has become the mother.

RITA: *(Comforting.)* Mum, Mum. Mum, Mum.

MARIA comes on from her place among the audience. She takes out her last cigarette, lights up and throws the pack away. Looks at them.

SOFIA: *(To PEDRO.)* He is a part of me.

PEDRO: A part?

SOFIA: One part.

RITA: *(Wanting to calm him in a loving way.)* Dad...

RITA brings her mother and father together. Tries to put her arms around them both, comfort them both at the same time.

RITA: *(Contd.)* Poor little Dad. Poor little Mum.

SOFIA: *(To PEDRO.)* You have your stories too.

PEDRO: I do.

Low tango music.

RITA lets go her parents, sets them in motion to the tango music. SOFIA and PEDRO start dancing, very slowly, their movements are at first barely discernible and slightly out of balance on the uneven surface.

21. Quite Calm

MARIA: *(To the audience, concerning the wedding dress that RITA is still wearing.)* Don't you think she should take that dress off now?

(To RITA.) Aren't you going to take that dress off now?

RITA: What?

MARIA: It's time to start.

RITA moves across to MARIA. SOFIA and PEDRO continue their cautious, almost exploratory dancing movements, their bodies remembering what their intellects have forgotten.

RITA: I don't know if I want to.

MARIA: You must.

MARIA helps RITA take off the wedding dress and hang it up. It rotates slowly on its own axis.

MARIA takes out one of the tiny sheets from the present she got from SOFIA (the one with the silk ribbon around it).

MARIA: *(Contd., reading.)* Don't leave me behind a closed door –
Let the door stand open –
Open the window wide –

The music becomes clearer. SOFIA and PEDRO continue to suggest a dance.

… and let me see the sky –
Let the wind embrace me.
As if it is you –

RITA: *(To the audience.)* Why am I crying?
I'm crying for Mum.
And for Dad.
For their love.
For all the sad things that happened.
For not belonging.
Always a foreigner. Always different.

PEDRO and SOFIA: two people who slowly and cautiously start dancing a perfectly normal, non-virtuoso tango. They are alive.

MARIA: *(Putting out her cigarette, talking to the audience and RITA.)*
I just wanted to walk down the street.

Stop and look around me, quite calm, while my heart beat calmly and well.

I wanted to see a flower closing at night,

watch it opening when daylight returned.

Wanted to see families picnicking in the park.

Kids playing on the beach.

To turn back after a person there was something special about,

sit down in a café and order a cold beer.

Drink it.

Change into clean trousers.

Buy a new pair of socks.

Walk up a hill and look out,

smell the spring coming,

let the wind play with my hair, let it swirl around my face:

I am here –

22. Tango

Rita picks things out from the under the large cloth, at length, she will remove it completely. Maria is still there, helping Rita. Sofia and Pedro dance. Rita and Maria talk together while sorting through the things they find: all the yellow newspapers are put in one place – as if exhibited to the audience. All the yarn is wound up and placed alongside the teddy bear and the three jerseys. Perhaps a flower grows somewhere out of this landscape, during this last scene.

The tiny slips of paper are laid in a pile right beside the audience or are perhaps given directly to audience members who are asked to take care of them for the time being.

Perhaps the wedding dress continues to turn on its axis – perhaps it gets more and more focus towards the end.

RITA: There's no point in keeping thinking about everything I should've asked about, taken responsibility for –

/

I regret not asking more questions, that I wasn't better at listening, that I didn't…

MARIA: None of that's your fault.

RITA: No.

MARIA starts clearing up again. RITA waits, looks at MARIA, wanting to get her to speak. Finally she asks:

RITA: Did you ever think you were going to die?

MARIA: *(Laughs.)* I guess you mean did I ever think I was going to survive?

RITA: Yes?

MARIA: Hope is strong. The capacity for survival enormous. I've never had a stronger feeling of being alive than there. Of being able to pull off the impossible. Talk about extreme sport. Don't need to go climbing in the Himalayas afterwards.

RITA laughs.

RITA: *(Excuses her laughter.)* Sorry.

MARIA: But I had decided to die. When they took us.

I didn't want to end up like the women I'd seen hanging there, naked. I'd rather die.

//

RITA: Go on.

MARIA: When they came for us at home and I knew there was no way out, I thought about making a run for it as we were led to the military car outside our house. They'd have shot me in the back. Then I'd be dead and it'd be over. But then they gave me one of the neighbour's kids and told me I had to carry him to the car. A tiny little boy. I couldn't let them kill him too, could I?

RITA: Did he survive?

MARIA: Yes. Well, I didn't run.

RITA: I mean – is he still alive today?

MARIA: He is, but, you know, he's not doing too well. He just kept crying and crying in prison. His mother had no calm to give him. And I wasn't allowed to comfort him. She kept a tight hold on him and he went on crying. For months. It was enough to make you go mad.

MARIA picks up a few tiny sheets; reads.

RITA: Where is he now?

MARIA: Who?

RITA: The boy.

MARIA: Oh, him. His mother took him and his brother with her to Europe. They're still there. Not everyone went back home when it was all over, you know.

RITA: *(About the sheets.)* What are we going to do with them?

MARIA: We can just give them back to your mother, can't we?

RITA: No, she said they should go on exhibition.

… Or shall we just throw them and be done with it?

MARIA: Some people say that everything should be thrown away. So that what you remember is all that's worth remembering.

RITA: What if I just remember pain? Then is pain all there is?

SOFIA and PEDRO dance a tango; the music is louder, they seem younger. MARIA performs a few cautious tango steps.

You know, I went to one of these places where they have tango, just recently. I hadn't heard any tango for years. Thought, that's cool, that was something my parents did when I was little and we were living in exile. And now I'd been told about this really good tango place. So I went. The show started and it was good.

And then I felt that I was crying. Why, I thought. Why cry now? Everything's fine –

/

I remember how wonderful Mum and Dad looked dancing together. On those times they couldn't get a babysitter, I was allowed to go with them. I used to crawl under one of the tables in the dance hall as the evening wore on. Curled up and looked out between the table-legs. Watched all the grown-ups dancing and Mum and Dad with their eyes so deeply fixed on one another.

//

RITA: *That* I remember.

23. What is to Happen with the Papers?

The music takes over.

SOFIA and PEDRO dance. MARIA too, alone. RITA talks to the audience; dances too perhaps.

At the exit, there are three boxes into which the tightly-written sheets may be placed.

On the boxes, it says:

- ☐ *SCHOOL CURRICULUM*
- ☐ *WASTE*
- ☐ *THE BOX IN THE CUPBOARD.*

Perhaps the actors tell the audience to put the papers into the respective boxes when they go, perhaps they discover it themselves.

Whatever – the music and the dance continue.

RITA watches her parents dancing; maybe she selects a dancing partner from the audience and gets more audience members to get up and dance. MARIA continues dancing alone, or maybe she too finds a partner. We'll see.

IT NEVER ENDS

WHY NOT BEFORE
Liv Heløe

Decision

1

He wakes up
Then his mother starts
clattering about in the kitchen
This happens every day He wakes up
Then she starts clattering
Recently he's started thinking about this That he wakes up
before
she starts clattering
It's as if he knows
while he's asleep
that she's going to start clattering
He wakes up to
avoid
being woken up
by her clattering

She rattles a basket of cutlery Bashes
clean saucepans together before
putting everything in the cupboard
Why does she do it

THE MOTHER: You never know what might've happened
during the night, dust could've fallen in, insects crept
about – We wouldn't want flies in our pans, would we – ?

But what kind of fly settles in
an upturned pan She clatters about to
wake him up Get him to
get up

And he gets up
Lowers his feet to the floor Goes
into the kitchen But he
doesn't answer when his mother asks

THE MOTHER: Did I wake you up – ?

He nips his phone off the charger Sits down at
the kitchen table
His mother says

THE MOTHER: Put your phone down, please –

But he doesn't put it down He
looks and looks at it As if there's something inside his
phone A riddle he has to
solve or a treasure he's supposed to find What
is he looking at

THE MOTHER: You won't find a job on the phone, you need
to get out – knock on a few doors – They've got a new girl
in at the shop on the corner, have you seen her?

He hasn't seen her

THE MOTHER: She's nice –

He hasn't seen her because he
doesn't go out What's he want to go out for
The only thing he looks at is
his phone

THE MOTHER: I bumped into someone from your old class,
he's working down at the ironmongers – at the shopping
centre, might that be something?

No No No

THE MOTHER: You have to start somewhere –

He's waiting for her to
go so he can
slink into bed Lay down Sleep
She says

THE MOTHER: You need to have applied for a job before the
week is out – you hear me?

He doesn't reply She puts her hand over the phone so
that he
has to look at her

THE MOTHER: If you don't, then I will – You understand? I'll
go down the centre, ask if you can have a job – If they say
yes, then that's it – you understand?

And then she leaves
The boy goes on looking at his phone like he's heard
nothing A video
A video of a
boy dancing on a manhole cover
A video
of a boy
Dancing
on a manhole cover
Why's he looking at this It's just some
random clip somebody's uploaded There's
millions of better videos Why does he know
every movement Every
step
The truth is
he doesn't know Even if he was tortured he wouldn't be
able to give a good answer as to why he
watches and watches
this video

Every day is like the next And the one before For almost
a year now
It's like
nothing exists outside the flat
He sleeps eats dreams
Sometimes he thinks he's going to die
in here He's even considered doing it himself Putting
an end to it all But he doesn't have
the courage Or strength Not the imagination either
perhaps Because
how would he do it
He doesn't think about
the future He just
exists
So what makes him
on this particular day take a decision that changes
everything
Is it because his mother said

THE MOTHER: I'll go down the centre, ask if you can have a
    job –

Or is it because he sees
his old classmate The one with the job at
the ironmongers going
past in the street In the ironmongers jacket The classmate
turns As if he
knows the boy's standing at the window He turns Lifts
an ironmongers arm Like he was going to
wave but he
doesn't wave He
draws his fingers across his own throat
smiling
Then he's gone

Or is it quite simply because
the time is ripe He can't
stay here any more
It's suddenly clear to him
Not one more day
And since the only thing he knows about is the video on
his phone he looks at that
Only now he's not watching
the dancing boy He's looking at
the sign on the café behind At
the name of the barber's shop to the
right of the café At the telephone box and
the tower towering over
everything else
And he decides he's
going there To the
manhole cover in
the city three thousand kilometres away

2

He's never booked a flight before Now
he does
Goes into his mother's room Finds her credit card in the
bedside table Goes back to
the computer Pays And he's
got a ticket

What does a person pack when they're leaving home and
don't know if they're coming back Not that he's
thinking he'll never come back Maybe then he'd've
done everything differently
Two pairs of trousers

Underwear T-shirts
Toothbrush
Wallet
The money he's got in the drawer
Mobile charger
Passport He nearly forgot that
A warm jumper
What else Nothing else

The plane leaves first thing in the morning but he
doesn't want to see his mother He puts on his
shoes Jacket Throws the bag over his shoulder Sees
the credit card on the table
Goes to put it back where
he found it but when he's
standing there
When he's standing there by his mother's
bedside table
he puts it in
his pocket instead

This thoughtlessness Or what else could you call it That
he
takes the credit card Gives him an unexpected
headache Because he's not a
thief He's impulsive and thoughtless Like a
calf as he's
walking towards the station
But as the distance becomes
greater
it begins bugging him
The credit card
His mother
That he's leaving her

He imagines her stopping at
the butchers and buying chicken Because he likes chicken
She walks home Opens the door She says

THE MOTHER: Hello –

But there's nobody there

THE MOTHER: Hello – ?

She opens the door to his room The bed is
empty She calls But he doesn't pick up Then she looks for
her credit card When she
can't find it she blocks
the account

He hasn't even written a
note And she's standing there with chicken because
he likes chicken
She who is scared of the dark Scared of being alone He's
suddenly burning with
shame And doubt
He's so unused to life that the simplest solution Putting
the credit card with a note in a postbox Doesn't even
occur to him No He
buries himself in self-reproach Like it's a
condition of life for him
to be unfree
But somewhere there's a voice that's saying
Not back Don't go back
And that's how he starts his looking for something
Something or another
to leave behind him A token A
teapot Something warming
A piece of jewellery

He sees his mother coming home Her
finding a teapot

THE MOTHER: Thank you –

A piece of jewellery

THE MOTHER: Thank you –

He looks up the street Down
A junkie's sitting slumped over on
the pavement Lost to the
world He's got a box beside him In it lie
three puppies all tangled up together
The boy squats down and
strokes one over its back It's warm
And it's not like it hits him as a
solution Or as a
good idea It's more like he
knows Like it's
predestined that this is
what he'll give his mother
Someone to talk to Someone to
make food for

He gives the junkie a little nudge of the shoulder
No reaction
He gets up Opens his wallet Has no idea of
what a dog should cost He thinks
About half
And he puts
half of his money in the junkie's pocket
Then he has to choose The littlest one lying
on top Who wants up and out The social one
sucking the tail of the littlest
Or the one

lying on its own Asleep
It'll be
that one
He lifts it up Then walks off No he
runs Carefully while holding the dog against his chest

The flat has become unfamiliar The one hour he has been
away has made an
ocean between him and the life he lived It's
incomprehensible that he was here just now

He finds a box Arranges a jumper in it Is about to
lay the pup in it but
puts her under his
T-shirt instead
Holds her against his heart
He leans back on his bed and
looks at the ceiling he has looked at
for days on end Now
he won't be looking at it any more
He feels her heart beating and he
feels his own and he's
quite calm
Then he lifts her into the box Puts the box on the bed
Goes into his mother's room and puts
the credit card in the bedside table
Is about to let himself out when he asks himself
What do I want with a key
He puts
the key on the table Heaves
his bag out the window and jumps out after it
He's on his way

3

He thinks about
free will If it exists
To what extent people choose
or if everything is determined
Not by god or fate but by
genes Circumstances
He wonders if the fact
he's now
leaving the place where he's grown up
is predetermined Or whether he's
chosen
He thinks
What does it mean that I don't have a father
Would everything have been different Would
I have been different
if I'd had a father
Would I have stayed here
Learned from him Become like him
Or what if I had a
brother A strong brother Would he have
protected me Given me
courage Would he have taught me to
fight Would I have been
stronger if I'd had a brother
He thinks about
the classmate that's got a job at the ironmongers
Would he have been
less brutal if he'd
grown up somewhere else If
his father was rich Would he have been different

Or would he have been the same
He thinks all this while sitting in
departures at the airport While watching people walk
past
Then he thinks
It makes no odds I'm leaving So it
makes no odds

He sends a message to his mother He writes
I'm fine

The street with the manhole cover

1

The people in a big city Do they look any different from
in a
small one
He can't quite manage to put his
finger on it Because it's not necessarily
the clothes or haircuts It's just as much an
attitude A way of
navigating A way of
avoiding looking
He notices it straight away in
arrivals Even those who arrived on
the same plane are kind of changed They're
going somewhere Have
direction No longer know the person beside them
He likes it
Yes
Being anonymous

On the train into the city he has this experience
A woman who's been sitting engrossed in her phone
suddenly leans forward Shows him – on the phone
A child tottering across a floor

WOMAN: That's my son, look – he's walking –

She doesn't want to
get to know him Doesn't want him to
say anything
Just show her child walking

WOMAN: See –

He learns something new about anonymity That it can
be used Perhaps he's the only person she'll
talk to today He thinks
No one would've done that back home
Shown their child to a
stranger
No
He looks at the woman But she's not looking at him
anymore

He studies a map and the metro network on his phone
There's
the café Where he's going
He plans a route with
three changes
ending up at a
yellow station
Yellow He takes that as a
good sign He likes yellow
A sign of what What does he think's
going to happen That
the boy on the video'll be standing outside the café
waiting for him No
But when he's on the escalator When he's
walking the streets towards the café he's checking out every
face Or Not every face He's checking out the young men
The slim young medium tall
men
Not him
Not him
Not him
Not him

215

And then he's there By
the café The barber's
The manhole cover where the boy danced
He walks over
in awe Stands there a
long while before putting his foot in the circle
It was
here he was coming
Now he's here

Is there anyone watching The café owner
The old man selling noodles across the street
The men on
the bench outside the barber's Does their
conversation stop
Are they wondering what he's up to
Or is he just one of a
thousand in this
street every day who do
things that only they
know why

He's hungry and
cuts across the street to
the noodle stand
The old man holds up two boxes
Large or small
Large of course

Once there were
trees in this street Now there are only stumps
left He sits down on one by the stand Eats while

looking over at the café
He must have stood right here The person who
filmed the boy He stood
on this stump one
warm afternoon and
filmed
For one reason or another he's
sure it was a he
Is it because there are only
men in the street Or is it because he
knows He
knows It was a boy
Filming his
friend

It gets dark
The old man closes his stand and
goes
The lights come on
Mopeds with young men Often
two on one whizz past
The café door opens and closes Opens and closes He
watches and watches Like a
child Doesn't think about
the day tomorrow or
what he's going to live on Not even where he's going to
sleep

About eleven he gets a
message

THE MOTHER: She's asleep in your room. I'm going to call
her Stella. A sign of life, please.

He writes back

I'm fine

THE MOTHER: Thank you. Good night.

He finds
cardboard outside the greengrocer's
The noodle stand's got big wheels He shoves
the cardboard and his bag underneath Wriggles
in
No one'll see him here But he sees
everything The café
The telephone box
He sees two
kiss as they go
each their own way
He's never seen that before Men
kissing He
holds round this little event like
something important As if he was
one of the two
Later he sees men openly doing
more than
kissing He notes it almost like
a research finding But it's the
kiss The sincerity That
touches him

The café closes and he sleeps Until
the road sweeper comes
He wriggles out Pees in an
alley
The café which was the
midpoint at night is just a closed door Now it's
the shops turn
Goods are delivered Signs put out

The old man arrives
Folds down the shutters Couples up
the electricity
A van stops Noodle mixes
are lugged into the stand and
the day's under way

The boy sits on
the stump watching
Customers buying
Men gathering
Some make calls from
the telephone box
Some run Some have
forgotten something
But no one dances on
the manhole cover

He's been here a whole day Has watched
everything happening and now it all begins
again

He finds a public toilet around the corner
Showers for the homeless
A coin wash in a cellar But he always
comes back to the stump
Later he looks back on these weeks
as very happy
A time without worry or
doubt

Is there anyone who
knows that he's
here in the street with the manhole cover Apart from
the old man in the noodle stand

He doesn't talk to
anyone Nobody seems to see him Who would
that be

One
There is one
that sees him

3

There's bad weather
coming
The old man bolts the shutters and leaves It's the same
for the shops Everything loose is taken
in The café closes
The boy packs
his telephone inside two plastic bags
Finds a small store that's still open Buys an
umbrella
When he pays he notices that
the note he hands over is his
last He can't make it
out Is certain
he's got more He turns his wallet
out It's empty
When the
first drops start falling he's sitting on
the stump in the empty street He takes his
clothes one by one
out of the bag Thinks he must have
some in reserve
And it's then When
everything he owns is strewn about him It's then

the heavens open
An explosion of water He
puts up his umbrella A
sudden gust turns it inside
out He
hurls it away Scrabbles after his
clothes Toothbrush Passport which is lying in apuddle
And then
when he's got everything back in
his bag and gets up An
advertising sign comes flying
through the air It's not big Not
heavy But it comes
from above and hits his head just
as he's getting up

MAN: You can't lie here, grab my hand – Here, grab my hand –
Let me take your bag – Come –
We can go to my place, it's not far –

Violence

Free will Does it exist
Or is everything determined
By genes Upbringing
Circumstance

MAN: My wife's away –

What brings him to this
flat with
a man he
thinks he's seen before but can't
quite place

MAN: Why'd you spread out everything everywhere, in the
middle of the street – ?

Is it the rain The sign that
hit him on the head

MAN: It's just a little cut –

Or the discovery that
the money he had has gone The confusion because he
didn't remember
giving the junkie half of it
Was it
the circumstances of that particular day
that meant he
wasn't so much
on his guard That he didn't

think about his saviour so
conveniently being there at
precisely the right moment

MAN: It's here – third floor –

Or would this have
happened anyway Because it was
predetermined Not by
god or fate But because he
is
the person he
is

MAN: You can hang your jacket there –

The room is
lounge and kitchen in one
The worktop's full of washing up

MAN: As I said, my wife's away –

Dining table Kid's chair Sofa
Picture of
the man and a
woman and a child on
the wall

MAN: Won't be a mo–

The man goes To
change perhaps
It's the first time for weeks
the boy's indoors It's like he's
forgotten how to
behave Should he take his shoes off
He takes them off

But he doesn't go
in Stands
just inside the door
Soaked
Where has he seen the man before He tries
to link the face with a
situation or a place but
finds nothing It feels like his brain is lame
There's a
training mat and weights in a
corner The man works out but
that doesn't mean anything

MAN: Why don't you take your jacket off – Here –

The man hands him some training pants and a T-shirt

MAN: Change into these –

Is he supposed to change here In front of the man
He takes off his jacket T-shirt Feels like a
skeleton in comparison with the man
He puts on the
dry T-shirt It's far too
big

He undoes his trousers Pulls them
down They're
wet Stick to
his thighs He
peels them off Picks up the training pants

MAN: Guess your underpants are wet too aren't they –

The boy turns away
Crouches inside

the T-shirt while he
pulls off his underpants
Is bending to pick up the training pants that are lying on
the floor when he feels
the man's hand
on his behind
He jumps
violently And
the man jumps because
the boy jumps

The boy does not look up He quickly pulls on
the training pants which are also
too big for him He has to
draw up the cords Tie them tight

When he turns round the man
is standing by the fridge opening a beer
Turns on the TV showing
the ravages of the storm
Cars with
water
up to
their windows People
wading
in their own cellars

MAN: You'd think it'd never rained before – that we were third
    world – so fucking amateurish, look at this –

He's not talking to
the boy He's talking to the air

MAN: And here she is – the minister bitch coming on to say
    everything's under control – Well let me tell you, bitch,
    that nothing – is under control –

The boy stands by the door
He could
reach
out
his hand Open the door and
go So easily He could just go
But his clothes
His passport
Where has the man put his bag

MAN: Won't you sit down – ? Sit down –

The boy walks over to the sofa
He regrets
every step All the same
he goes to the sofa
Sits down

MAN: Better than the noodle stand, eh – better than
cardboard and tarmac –

He has seen him Under
the noodle stand

MAN: P'r'aps you thought nobody saw you – ?

He changes channels Soap Adverts
Porn
He leaves the porn on Three
men take a
woman in turn In
all her openings

The boy would do
anything not to
have to
watch With

this man But he's
incapable
of getting up He
stares at a
picture beside
the TV A photograph of
a child The same child as in
the picture by
the door
Then the man sits down
beside him
Puts his hand on
his thigh
The boy tries to
move his thigh away But
the hand follows and
suddenly the hand is a claw Holding the spindly thigh in
an
iron grip Jerks so the boy
is suddenly on his back The man sits
over him And
hits him
Hits
and
hits
He hits
And hits
And hits

He is walking in a
wood Carrying the little
dog Then it wants to
walk itself He puts it down and it
leads the way Like it knows where they're going But they
don't get anywhere Just
deeper into the darkness
He stops but
the dog keeps going
He lies down Sees light above
the trees That must be
the sky
It's good to
lie like this
He doesn't understand why he's been
struggling and struggling to
go forward Why should
he

Then
the dog is back
Licking his face
He
lifts up a hand to stroke it but the dog
is gone Where'd
it go He
opens his eyes and peers at his hand
It's
red

The boy does not understand that the blood on his hand
is his
He doesn't know where he is
It's like everything's in a fog

He lifts his head Then
it spews out Vomit
He sits up
Throws up again
He's dizzy
Makes out a shape
Lifts an arm and holds it in front
of his head like a shield
The shape says something What is it
he's saying

MAN: Get up!

The boy musters
all his strength

MAN: Go to the bathroom –

Where is the bathroom
He walks towards something
that might be a door Where's
all the fog from

He feels
desperately sick His head
whines and he smashes
his chin on the sink as he
collapses to the
floor

A WOMAN: Hello –

    Someone is slapping
    his face

A WOMAN: Hello –

    A woman

A WOMAN: Wake up –

    He opens his eyes to bring a stop to it

A WOMAN: Get up – Is this your bag –

    His bag

A WOMAN: Take it –

    His bag

A WOMAN: Take it – Get up - Go – Don't lie down, go –

    She pulls him up He's
    dizzy

A WOMAN: And now go – Go –

    He takes a step Another
    He goes through the entry How
    did he get here

A WOMAN: Keep going – don't lie down

    What a fuss

A WOMAN: Go –

    And then she's gone He
    goes Because she said he should Holds onto

his bag Because she said he should
hold on to it
He doesn't know where He's just going
And it's either because the street
slopes this way Or because he's drawn towards the sun Or
because it's
predetermined
He goes straight back to the stump
There he sits down and when the old man comes
he faints

The tailor

So what happens When
the noodle seller finds the malnourished boy Almost
beaten to death Does he
raise the alarm Does he call
the police
No
He painstakingly bends down Feels for his pulse
Turns him over on
one side and waits for
the noodle van With the driver's help he gets
the boy into
the van and they drive to the street where the noodle-
seller lives Stop outside a little workshop A tailor's

The tailor comes out They carry
the boy into
the back room of the workshop

The tailor rings his nephew who studies medicine The
nephew thinks the boy must be taken to a doctor The
tailor
cancels his day's work Gets the boy to
hospital They sew a cut in his head and put him through a
drum They find no
lasting damage The medicine is
peace and quiet

Three months he lies in the dark in the back room
The tailor gives him

tea and food In the
evenings the noodle-seller comes They
eat in the workshop The boy
sits at the table for a while Then goes back to lie down
The tailor and the noodle-seller say
good night and
disappear in
the upper floors
He sleeps a lot Tires
quickly Gets
headaches if he
thinks
The tailor says

THE TAILOR: Don't brood. Imagine you're a dog lying by the
stove, it doesn't make plans –

He thinks about the pup in the box that didn't
crawl about Just
slept

Only after several
weeks does he charge up his phone Then the messages
from his mother come
streaming in

THE MOTHER: Where are you? Has something happened?

THE MOTHER: Haven't you got any money? Shall I send some?

THE MOTHER: Please, let me know you're there. Please.

He writes
Everything's fine
She answers straight away

THE MOTHER: Thank God.

It's winter
The boy is up for longer at a stretch
One day when
the tailor's out he tidies the reels Another day the needles
And one day He has seen the tailor do it loads of times He attaches
the arms to a smoking jacket Just with pins and he's
thinking of taking them off again before
the tailor gets back but when he
sees the jacket
with the arms on
Like it's been given
life Like it can
stroll out into the world
He leaves it as it
is

The tailor comes back
The tailor says

THE TAILOR: Did you do this?

The boy regrets it
immediately In a
moment he sees himself go out
the door Down the street and away
Where shall he
go

THE TAILOR: Come here – If you push the pin in a bit further
here – then it's perfect, you see?

It's perfect
At a

stroke the day has meaning
That day and the day after From now on
he follows everything the tailor does Sucks it up Practices til
his eyes flicker and he has to
lie down
Then he's
up again Taking measurements Learning About
cut Fit Movement
The tailor says he has
talent

THE TAILOR: You're a born tailor – Why didn't you come
  before?

Why didn't you come before
Is he saying that to
please the boy or does he mean it
The boy lives there like a son
Eats with the tailor and the noodle-seller
Sleeps in
the back room Hears
people walking past on the street but
the door is properly locked

3

It turns to spring The boy and the tailor sew
summer suits
It turns to summer They plan
autumn jackets
In the autumn they sew
winter coats
Then the spring comes and it all starts
again

He doesn't often go out That's to say
Not without a purpose He runs the errand and comes
back
One day he sees
the man Knows
immediately that it's him Even
from behind at a fair distance
He's wearing
a uniform with a logo for a
security company on the back Of course He's a security guard
Was in the street with the manhole cover
Saw him on the stump Decided to pick him up
The boy shivers despite
the sun shining
He turns straight back
to the workshop where he spends the rest of the day in
bed

THE TAILOR: What's up?

The tailor asks

THE TAILOR: Don't catch cold –

He has of course asked Both him and the noodle-seller
about
what happened
But they've never got an answer

Two years pass
Three Four
Many of the tailor's customers prefer
the boy He's
quick and precise

A couple of times a

month he exchanges messages with his mother The boy
might write that
The weather's nice
His mother answers

THE MOTHER: Here too. Spring at last. Stella soaking up the sun.

With a picture of Stella attached
eyes closed
Occasionally the boy sits on the
metro of a Sunday
While whooshing through the
city he looks at his phone and sometimes
he leans
forward Stretches out a hand with his
phone and shows a fellow passenger
Stella asleep

PASSENGER: Is that your dog?

Stella playing

PASSENGER: She's so sweet – !

Stella dancing
Is it such That after these fleeting meetings he is
content Can he live the rest of his life
like this
He doesn't think about it He
lives from
day to day Misses
nothing

4

Three new years pass The old man has

retired and he's the
district's tailor

He's had
invitations To parties Events
But he's never
gone
He still sleeps in the back room

And so his life might have continued but for
a message one day
ticking in from his mother She writes

THE MOTHER: I've always thought never to ask you to come
home. I've always thought you'll come if you want to. But
I haven't been myself recently. The doctor says I need
to have a lump removed. I'm being operated on in three
days.
Can you come home?

He looks at
the telephone like he doesn't
understand
Then he gets up
Walks to the metro
Jumps in a
carriage Changes lines Changes again
Not until late at night does he get home
The two old men are waiting at the door

THE TAILOR: Where have you been?

He opens his computer and books a flight
For the second time in his life

Back

1

The dog barks
Then the door opens and there's
a person there Bending with a
hand in the collar so that the dog won't leap forward

It's his mother Of course But so
little So thin
Grey-haired
She's sent pictures of the dog Never her
self

She straightens
her back Lifts her gaze and looks him in the face

THE MOTHER: You're so handsome –

She lifts her hand But
doesn't touch him

THE MOTHER: You're so handsome –

2

The stove is
new The curtains Otherwise
everything's like before
His mother says lots has happened The streets in the city
centre have been
changed The park has got a fountain
But everything is

just as it was

She's going to have a cyst removed Several times
she says

THE MOTHER: I'm not scared –

But the bag with her
toiletries is ready
He shows her pictures
Suits he's made

THE MOTHER: To think that you're a tailor – I'd never've
believed it –

The noodle-seller by
his stand

THE MOTHER: Is that your neighbour –

The old tailor with a cup of tea

THE MOTHER: So you don't have a girlfriend?

The dog is lying by the stove

Evening comes He
opens the door to his old room
It's like a
museum
Tidied Washed But everything's there
Most of all
the smell
He puts his case down by
the desk He'll be looking after
the dog for the three days she'll
be gone No
more no less

When he goes to bed he has the window
wide open All the same At
night he dreams that he's drowning

3

His mother goes through the
dog's walks and meals Then she takes her bag and
goes
He longs for
the workshop Puts his
air ticket on the table like
insurance of his going
back

He goes where his mother
said
Three blocks away Round the playground Past the school
and home
The dog decides where they
stop How long they
stand

He doesn't think about everything he's
been through in these
streets
How he
avoided the playground so he didn't
meet anyone Or how he When he was
caught Laughed He
doesn't think about that
He's
walking there because
his mother told him to

walk there

The dog stops He
looks into the schoolyard where a
man
is hosing the tarmac
He doesn't think about
everything that happened in this schoolyard In
the toilets In the stairways His head
is empty
But when the man
turns round He sees that
it's his old
classmate
The one who got
a job at
the ironmonger's It's
him who's
hosing the tarmac in the schoolyard and the boy For he
suddenly feels like a
boy Turns away
Doesn't want to be seen
He walks on But
the dog hangs back He
pulls Drags her
away and after a few feet she gives in

He goes from
room to room Grabs a
cup off the worktop Hurls it against
the wall
Catches a
glimpse of himself in
the bathroom mirror and

slams the door so hard that
something falls down
Then he sees
the rubbish bin He
lifts it up Clasps it like he wants to
crush it But he doesn't
crush it
He
walks Out
the door Down the street
Ploughs through a
school-class out on a trip On to
the gate where he sees
his old classmate coiling up the hose He
walks over to him
looks him in the eye and
empties the rubbish bin between them

Then he does something he's
never done before He
goes running
The dog with him
He thinks
Do I decide to run Or
do I run because I can't
do anything else Does
fate hold me on a
lead like I'm holding the dog
Am I
when all's said and done
like the dog Lifted out of a basket Put down at some
random place And then this place
Along with the abilities

and weaknesses I'm born with
determines every hour I live
Is that how it is

He thinks about
the weeks by the noodle stand
The brute who
wound him in
He chose
me
he thinks Because it was written all over me
I am
condemned Take
me
He thinks about
the days by the sewing machine
The nights in the back room
The workshop appears like a
prison he's
chosen to enter A
darkness he
couldn't have chosen away
He looks at
his hands and asks
Why did I become a tailor
Was it simply because I
fetched up in that workshop Could I
have become something
else
Architect
Mathematician
Even my mother
can't understand why I'm a tailor

Later he walks
restlessly round the flat
He thinks
If I haven't chosen to be a tailor Why should
I carry on with it Why
sew suits when
the world is full of clothes
It's completely
pointless
He looks at the air ticket on
the kitchen table Wants to tear it to
pieces but he
doesn't
He thinks
So poor and cowardly that I can't even
manage to tear up a ticket
He wants to scream but he
can't manage it
He reaches a hand into the
kitchen cupboard where he remembers
his mother used to keep a bottle There
it stands Like it
always has
Halfway
down the bottle he thinks

If
free will doesn't exist
then I can't be held
responsible
for my actions
If I stab my neighbour
with a knife If I

drive a car into a crowd of people If I
detonate a bomb at an airport
No one can blame me
For it
is determined beforehand

And so

He's waiting for his mother to return home
Sleeping poorly
Barely eating

There's a knife lying on the side
He thinks It shouldn't be lying there like that On
the side It should be in the drawer
He thinks he should
put it in the
drawer but he doesn't and as time
passes he begins to think it's
lying there for a reason and he gets
scared
He imagines his mother
coming That she asks again if he hasn't got a
girlfriend That she asks him
to stay He
imagines
stabbing her with the knife In that
thin belly

He packs Puts out
water for the dog Lifts his suitcase through the window and
is about to clamber after it when
his arm suddenly shoots out and grabs the knife
Puts it in his jacket pocket
Then he's on his way

He's sitting in departures outside
the security control
Two guards look at him He thinks
What if they come over
What if they talk to me
But they don't come over And
his eyes close

When he wakes In a minute or
quarter of an hour What then
Will he get rid of the knife
Go through the security control Eat for the first time in
ages and make plans for the
workshop and the future
Or will he stay in departures
Wander about until
the guards approach him and he
cracks and everything comes to an end

Is it determined beforehand By
genes Circumstances
The dream he has asleep in
departures What does it mean
The dream is like this

He's sitting on the metro Passing
stop after
stop Until he comes to a
yellow station
Here he gets off He

doesn't know why

But when he's standing on the escalators When he's
walking in

the streets he's checking out the

slim

medium tall men

Not him

Not him

Not him

Not him

WATCHING SHADOWS
Hans Petter Blad

Characters

RAKEL
ANDRÉ: Rakel's boyfriend
ELISABETH: her best friend
JACOB: Elisabeth's boyfriend
YLVA: friend
EMBLA: friend
INGER: Rakel's little sister
YOUNG PEOPLE

Scene 1

The stage is dark. Enter ELISABETH, alone, in light, summer clothes.

ELISABETH: I don't know.

Pause.

I said I don't know, it's true, I don't remember.

Pause.

Because I was dancing.

Pause.

No, not the whole evening, I'd arranged to meet someone, and so we went –

Pause.

Italian, yes.

Pause.

No, I have a boyfriend at home in Norway.

Pause.

OK. From the beginning then.

Pause.

I met Paolo at a *gelateria,* he bought me an ice cream, then we went for a walk along the beach, and then we met his friends. We had drinks, and –

Pause.

No, not much. I'm not very fond of drinking.

Pause.

Yes, I'm eighteen, I can do what I want.

Pause.

No, I didn't see Rakel at all. I didn't see her before we arrived where we all used to meet up, a night club or a disco. Maybe I had a little bit more to drink there –

Pause.

No, I'm not sure, not very much, I wasn't drunk, not very drunk, I spent most of the time on the dance floor with Paolo.

Pause.

No, not with anyone else, just with Paolo.

Pause.

No, we're not together, I told you, I have a boyfriend at home in Norway.

Pause.

I'm sorry. I didn't mean to –

Pause.

OK, I'll continue. I danced for ages, was sweaty and tired, and must've been a little bit drunk, needed some air, and Paolo wanted to have a cigarette, so we went outside. He ordered a couple of beers, and I went straight out onto the street to wait for him outside, there were a number of people we knew there, a few Norwegians, mostly girls, but a few Italian boys too, we liked hanging out together.

Pause.

That's when I saw her. I saw Rakel.

Pause.

Yes, I'm absolutely positive.

Pause.

She was wearing that airy light dress she always wore, and she got brown so quickly, she was really beautiful, she looked like she normally did, only perhaps –

Pause.

No, I don't know –

Pause.

Perhaps even happier, or more, how can I put it, fired up, than she usually was. She was radiant. She was standing on her own in the street, I looked at her, we waved at each other, and afterwards I thought how strange that was, that we waved, in a slightly odd way, we were facing each other, and waved goodbye. Then she turned around and disappeared.

Pause.

I think, I think –

Scene 2

YOUNG PEOPLE move in a long row with their eyes fixed on the ground as if they are looking for something. One of them is ELISABETH. They move slowly, with short steps, anxious lest they should miss anything important. Every time they find something, they run over to a small table and deposit the item there. Then return to their place in the line. They continue moving forward with the tiniest of footsteps.

ELISABETH: I'm absolutely certain – it was there, at the disco, that I saw her for the last time. For my own part, I just disappeared into the music. I lost all sense of time and place and could hardly recognise myself. No, wait –

The music is heard and ELISABETH begins to dance immediately, though cautiously, almost for herself.

ELISABETH: Or, no – then I found out she had disappeared. I was on the dance floor, it was so hot, so crowded, I was suffocating, I had to get some air and went out with – I went outside. That's how it was. And then I saw her. Then I saw her for the last time. I don't just think so, I'm certain.

YOUNG PERSON 1: She went down this way, towards the beach, and disappeared.

YOUNG PERSON 2: She was with this guy, I'd never seen him before. He wasn't from round here, a foreigner perhaps. They were arguing, and he was terribly angry. I don't know what they were arguing about, I was drunk too.

YOUNG PERSON 3: He was much older than her.

YOUNG PERSON 4: She got into a taxi, the driver – it shouldn't be difficult to find him. He looked – perfectly ordinary.

YOUNG PERSON 5: It surprised me that she was kissing someone, she wasn't really the type, but she was pretty drunk, never seen her so drunk before, but now she was drunk as hell and hanging on somebody's arm, maybe it was one of the Scandinavian guys.

Pause.

I'd recognise him if I saw him, I think.

Pause.

But I hadn't seen him before.

The music is turned off. The YOUNG PEOPLE continue walking in their line. If they find anything suspicious, they put it on the table.

YOUNG PERSON 1: What can I say? She was a perfectly ordinary Scandinavian girl.

YOUNG PERSON 2: Pretty. Fair hair. Always very happy.

YOUNG PERSON 3: I spoke to her a long time one evening. In Italian.

Pause.

She had only been here a few days and she was speaking Italian. Not perfect, but not far off either.

Pause.

I've had English for years and can still hardly say a word. But she, she spoke fluently –

YOUNG PERSON 4: She was pretty, what else can I say? Just like all the others, perhaps just a bit more stuck-up. She didn't want to, how can I put it, she –

Pause.

She didn't want to hook up with anyone, she just smiled and liked everybody equally, at the same time, no one was good enough for her, it's –

Pause.

Anyway, she wasn't my type.

YOUNG PERSON 5: Rakel thought she was smarter than everyone else. Probably was too. I liked her. She was interested in politics, it was the only thing we ever talked about.

YOUNG PERSON 6: She wanted to change the world.

YOUNG PERSON 7: Rakel liked talking to us because we shared the dream.

Pause.

About a different world, rather –

The young Italians exit. ELISABETH is left standing alone.

ELISABETH: Rakel disappeared in a dress she'd used a thousand times. No make-up, no done-up hair, no jewellery.

Pause.

She had almost nothing with her, all the same –

Pause.

We looked for her for days, her and her things. We found so many strange things. Earrings, money, a watch, a wallet, sandals, and for everything we found, I had to say if it could have been hers.

Pause.

I was asked to say, if the things we found had any significance, or if they were just ordinary things.

Pause.

This isn't Rakel's.

Pause.

This is Rakel's.

Pause.

This is Rakel.

ELISABETH holds up different small objects and, lastly, a postcard.

ELISABETH: In her room, at her place, the police found a postcard she never sent.

Pause.

It was "suspicious" and I had to translate it for them.

Pause.

First I read it out in Norwegian, and then I translated it as best I could.

ELISABETH reads from the postcard.

ELISABETH: Dear Inger, my dear little sister. I thought I'd write you a postcard since people hardly ever do that anymore. *Cartolina* and *francobollo* is what postcard and stamp are in Italian. It's lovely to be here, and I'm learning loads of Italian, but some days I'm so sad I can't manage anything else but to cry. Bu what am I going to do with all these words, I don't want to talk to anyone, or see anyone, I don't want to –

Pause.

Some words are crossed out, in black, they're impossible to read.

Pause.

At the top of the card there's a date.

Pause.

She wrote it the day before she disappeared.

Scene 3

ANDRÉ is walking, lost in his own thoughts. He takes out an envelope, pulls out the letter from inside, reads it to himself.

Enter EMBLA and YLVA. They see ANDRÉ but do not go over to him. When they speak, they speak quietly.

EMBLA: There's André.

YLVA: Yeah. He looks –

> *Pause.*

> He looks terribly sad.

EMBLA: I think he's always looked sad.

> *Pause.*

> It's like he's always walking around thinking seriously about something – *(pause)* important, or deep, in his own world.

YLVA: We can't just stand here. Pretend we can't see him. We have to go over to him. Tell him what we feel, that we feel sorry for him, how much we all love Rakel, that of course she'll be back, everything will be alright, and –

EMBLA: Won't that be a bit much? If we both –

YLVA: Ok? D'you think that –

EMBLA: Yes, I think that'd be best.

> *Pause.*

> That only one of us goes over.

> *Pause.*

I can talk to him.

YLVA: Ok, but –

EMBLA: I'll talk to you later.

Pause.

Relax, I'll tell you everything afterwards. Don't be cross.
It's not anything I'm doing for myself, it's for his sake,
not mine.

*Exit YLVA. EMBLA goes over to ANDRÉ. The moment he sees her,
he puts the letter back in the envelope, which he puts in the back
pocket of his trousers.*

EMBLA: You look sad.

ANDRÉ: Embla, sorry, I didn't see you coming –

EMBLA: No, that's not what I meant, that you shouldn't
look sad.

Pause.

Of course you're upset.

Pause.

Is Rakel still –

ANDRÉ: Missing, yes. There's nothing new.

EMBLA: Have you spoken to her mother, or her father, have
you spoken with Inger, to be so young and maybe to have
lost, I can't bear the thought of it –

ANDRÉ: Yes, I should have but. No.

Pause.

I think it's difficult.

EMBLA: It looked like you were reading something.

ANDRÉ: Yeah?

EMBLA: Have you had a letter from her?

ANDRÉ: No.

EMBLA: I thought it looked like you were reading, maybe
    I didn't see properly.

(He does not answer.) Do you want to come down to the beach?

ANDRÉ: The beach, I don't know.

Pause.

It's nice of you to ask, but –

EMBLA: We don't need to go in. We can just talk.

Pause.

It's not wrong of you, just to go down to the beach, or go
for a swim if you want to.

Pause.

Come on!

They leave.

Scene 4

*INGER, Rakel's sister, is lying on the beach or jetty. The sound of waves
and the sea can be heard.*

*Enter EMBLA and ANDRÉ walking; they see her. Go over to her, towering
over her, exchange glances. When they speak, they speak quietly.*

ANDRÉ: Is she asleep?

EMBLA: Yes.

ANDRÉ: Looks like it.

EMBLA: *(Leans over her.)* Yes, she's asleep. Her hair's wet. Must have just had a swim then gone to sleep in the sun.

ANDRÉ: She knows what's happened?

EMBLA: Yes – she must do. They must have told her.

ANDRÉ: Shall we go a bit further along?

EMBLA: No. Can't we sit here until she wakes up.

EMBLA and ANDRÉ sit down.

EMBLA: It must be terrible. Losing your girlfriend.
Or – maybe losing her.

ANDRÉ: I'm sure she's going to come back.

EMBLA: Yes, of course. But all the same. All the same –

She puts her hand on his.

EMBLA: You have to think about yourself too.

ANDRÉ: Um –

EMBLA: Yes? What is it?

ANDRÉ: No.

Pause.

I don't know if –

EMBLA: You can say it.

ANDRÉ: I –

EMBLA: What?

ANDRÉ: It's not true. It's not true that Rakel and I are boyfriend and girlfriend. She broke up before she left. But she didn't want me to tell anyone.

Pause.

Then it would look like she'd just gone to Italy to get off with some other bloke, but that wasn't why.

Pause.

She said.

EMBLA: But, I.

Pause.

I thought you two were alright together.

ANDRÉ: So did I. I was sure, but she said it was all her fault and that she was just going to make me unhappy.

EMBLA: Aw – *(Hugs him)* Was –

ANDRÉ: What?

EMBLA: Is that why you haven't spoken to her mum and dad?

(ANDRÉ nods.) But, that might mean that, that she –

Pause.

I think maybe you should tell her parents. Or the police.

ANDRÉ: Yes. Probably.

EMBLA: If you interpret it in the worst possible way.

ANDRÉ: Yeah. I know.

EMBLA: No. No! I refuse to, of course not!

Pause.

She'd never do anything like that.

INGER turns over in her sleep, stretches and changes position, but doesn't appear to wake up.

EMBLA: But it's a bit strange that she split up with her boyfriend, with you, then left for a language course in Italy, where she disappeared the day before she was supposed to fly home.

Pause.

Without any message except a cryptic unfinished postcard she never sent. To her little sister. According to Elisabeth.

Pause.

Should we wake her up?

ANDRÉ: Hope she hasn't heard –

EMBLA: Inger.

(Louder.) Inger!

INGER sits up. Looks at them.

INGER: I fell asleep in the sun.

Pause.

Isn't there anyone else here?

EMBLA: No.

INGER: I remember now, they went home, the others. I said I wanted to be on my own for a while.

EMBLA: Yes. You alright?

ANDRÉ: We can follow you home.

INGER: Yes, I'm just tired. I'm upset and tired and then I can't get to sleep at night, none of us at home are sleeping, everyone sits awake, expecting the phone to ring, that someone'll ring, and say – we've found her, she's fine, she's come back. So we sleep in the middle of the day when we should be awake.

ANDRÉ: She'll come back.

INGER: Will she?

ANDRÉ: Maybe I shouldn't say it, but I know it, I know, that Rakel will come back.

EMBLA: How old are you now, Inger?

INGER: Soon be fourteen.

EMBLA: You seem older, more grown up.

INGER: Everyone says that. That I'm mature for my age, as if I'd grown specially much now, this summer.

ANDRÉ: And your parents?

INGER: My dad's travelling down to help look for her.

Pause.

If he hasn't already left.

(Looks up.) Maybe he's on his way to Italy now.

ANDRÉ: And your mum?

INGER: She talks about you mostly. She feels sorry for you, she says, it must be awful.

ANDRÉ: Yes. Say hello from me will you?

INGER: I think she'd prefer it if you came by for a visit. Since your boyfriend and girlfriend, she said.

ANDRÉ: Yes. Of course. Can't you say hello to your mum for me and say –

Pause.

That I'll come. For a visit.

Pause.

And tell her not to worry.

Pause.

Your dad'll find her.

INGER: Mum says that too.

Pause.

That it'll be alright.

Scene 5

JACOB and ELISABETH, he in Norge, she in Pietrasanta, Italy.

JACOB: Hi, it's me. Jacob, your boyfriend.

ELISABETH: Yes. I know, I haven't forgotten you.

JACOB: When are you coming home?

ELISABETH: Don't know. I should have flown home yesterday but it feels wrong, just leaving.

JACOB: Is it because of her you're staying?

ELISABETH: Yes.

JACOB: OK, are you sure about that?

ELISABETH: Of course, what else would it be?

Pause.

I'm waiting for her. I want there to be someone here, someone she knows, when she comes back.

JACOB: She's not coming back.

Pause.

She's not coming back.

ELISABETH: And you know that? What nobody else knows, what –

JACOB: Perhaps, sometimes, I know more than you think.

ELISABETH: Listen, I have to –

JACOB: *(Interrupts.)* Who were you dancing with?

ELISABETH: I don't know, I danced and danced and –

JACOB: Is that why you didn't want me to come?

ELISABETH: I never said that you couldn't –

JACOB: Yes, you did, that's exactly what you said, I want to be alone, you said, I want to go on my own, without you.

Pause.

You didn't want me to come.

Pause.

And look what's happened.

Pause.

It could have been you.

Haven't you got that?

ELISABETH: No!

Pause.

I wanted to travel alone because I wanted to learn Italian.
I wanted to speak Italian, not speak Norwegian with you.

Pause.

Why would I travel all the way to Italy just to be together
with you the whole time and speaking Norwegian the
whole time?

JACOB: And now you've spoken Italian, with your Italians.

ELISABETH: Yes.

JACOB: Were they friendly? Like you dreamed about? And
have you been –

ELISABETH: Jacob –

JACOB: I can't bear talking with you any more now. It
wouldn't surprise me if it's because of you she's gone.

ELISABETH: I promise, I promise I haven't done anything
wrong. Do you believe me?

Pause.

Don't you believe me?

JACOB: *(Stretches out his hand towards her, as if they were in the
same room.)* I believe you.

*JACOB leaves, ELISABETH leaves, in the opposite direction. A few
YOUNG PEOPLE are waiting for her.*

Scene 6

EMBLA is sitting on the steps outside the local constable's office. Enter YLVA.

YLVA: What are you doing here?

EMBLA: I'm not doing anything –

YLVA: Have you been into the police?

EMBLA: No, of course not.

YLVA: But what are you doing here then?

> *Pause.*

> Waiting for someone?

> *Pause.*

> It's André. You're waiting for André.

EMBLA: No, I'm not.

YLVA: Does he know anything? Has he told you anything?

EMBLA: Can't you just go!

YLVA: Ok. I'm going, if –

> *Pause.*

> If you tell –

EMBLA: That's blackmail.

YLVA: Then I'll stay then.

> *YLVA sits down beside EMBLA*

EMBLA: Ok. I'll tell, it was supposed to be a secret.

Pause.

Rakel broke off just before she went.

Pause.

She broke up and then left for a language course in Italy for four weeks.

Pause.

Then she disappeared, the day before she was supposed to fly home.

Enter ANDRÉ.

YLVA: Ok, but –

Pause.

Why's he telling all of this to you?

Pause.

How come you've become such good friends all of a sudden?

EMBLA: Don't say anything, to anyone, please –

Pause.

Hi, André –

Pause.

Any news?

ANDRÉ: No.

ANDRÉ, EMBLA and YLVA sit silently beside each other until JACOB appears.

JACOB: You going down to the beach?

Pause.

So what're you doing here?

Pause.

I've talked to Elisabeth.

Pause.

She. She's fine. I was to say hello. To everybody.

Pause.

Any news? I'm sure Rakel, yeah, that everything's fine.

Pause.

That there's no reason for us to be scared.

Well, I'm going to have a swim.

EMBLA: Yeah, why do we always imagine the worst?

Pause.

What if the opposite's happened?

Pause.

What if she's living one big adventure and we're standing here, worrying about her for no reason at all.

Pause.

What if she's never had such a good time?

JACOB: I doubt that.

EMBLA: What if she's found the love of her life?

JACOB: Whatever, I can't be bothered brooding about every hour of the day.

YLVA: If you disappear and don't come back after 24 hours, you're gone forever. And, those who disappear, want to disappear.

Pause.

That's what's most likely, that that's *the truth*.

Pause.

Young people disappear all the time.

Pause.

Think of a town the size of, well, a town of almost one hundred thousand people, consisting only of a young people, a town which, from one day to another, just disappears, where all the people simply went missing, for good.

Pause.

That's the reality in Europe today, in the world. Young, troubled people get up, get dressed, rush out, turn their backs on everything and disappear. In one way or another. And then they're gone for good.

Pause.

They want to get away, from all this, more than anything else –

ANDRÉ: How can you know that, Ylva, how can you know that for sure?

YLVA: It's not difficult to find out. You only have to google it. You just need to spend five minutes of your valuable time to find out.

Pause.

Instead of –

EMBLA: What?

YLVA: Being here with us.

The music from the discothèque where RAKEL disappeared can be heard. They dance. Everyone. Enter INGER. Looks at them. It goes quiet.

INGER: What are you doing here?

JACOB: Nothing.

Pause.

There's nothing we can do.

Pause.

Not to be cynical or anything but –

Pause.

The summer'll soon be over and –

Pause.

I've done nothing apart from wait for something that's never happened.

Scene 7

EMBLA and YLVA are alone on the beach, drying their hair maybe, or getting dressed – throwing summer dresses over their swimming costumes or standing there changing.

EMBLA: *(To the others, just leaving.)* See you tomorrow.

(To YLVA.) Wait. Can you keep a secret, a – *(pause)* – really big secret?

YLVA: Of course.

EMBLA: Well now that I've gone that far.

Pause.

I've fallen in love with –

YLVA: No!

EMBLA: No, don't be angry –

YLVA: But what if –

EMBLA: There's André. I'll just have to take it.

Pause.

I'll have to take it.

YLVA leaves. EMBLA is left standing alone. Then ANDRÉ comes to view.

EMBLA: Can you talk?

ANDRÉ: Yes.

Pause.

You didn't say anything to Ylva?

Pause.

About. Rakel.

Pause.

Or about us.

EMBLA: No. But – we haven't done anything wrong, she broke up, you're not together, not now anyway, regardless of what's happened, and –

Pause.

So what did they say? The police?

ANDRÉ: They said it was right of me to come.

EMBLA: They weren't angry with you, that you hadn't come earlier?

ANDRÉ: No.

Pause.

I could feel it though.

EMBLA: That?

ANDRÉ: To them it was obvious. Why she'd broken up before going on holiday. So she could find a new boyfriend. Down there.

EMBLA: So what did you say?

ANDRÉ: I said.

Pause.

I said I thought that if she had disappeared, then she had killed herself. She's not the sort of person to go with somebody she doesn't know or who'd let herself be tricked into taking some dope, or who – no, if anything's happened to her, it's because she wanted it to happen.

Pause.

Ylva's right.

That if she's disappeared, it's because she wanted to.

EMBLA: Whatever happens.

Pause.

And now I'm almost pleased for what's happened. No! I didn't mean it like that. I gotta dash.

EMBLA goes back to YLVA.

EMBLA: It was André.

YLVA: Yeah?

EMBLA: I don't think anyone understands how difficult it is.

Pause.

For André.

Pause.

Of course it's horrible for us. And for Inger, but she's so young, so full of optimism. She –

Pause.

probably thinks her sister'll be coming back.

Pause.

Whereas we know that's not true.

Pause.

We don't know if she's run away for good, found the love of her life or is lying chained up in some fucking –

YLVA: No, I don't want –

EMBLA: to think –

YLVA: the thought –

EMBLA: through –

YLVA: even.

EMBLA: I don't either.

YLVA: I pray to God that she'll come back.

Pause.

It's stupid.

Pause.

I don't even believe in God.

Scene 8

ELISABETH and INGER, in Italy and in Norway.

INGER: Is it alright if I'm calling? It's Rakel's little sister.

ELISABETH: Inger!

Pause.

Yes. Of course it's alright.

INGER: I tried calling Dad but he didn't pick up the phone.

Pause.

Have you spoken to him?

ELISABETH: He's out looking for Rakel.

Pause.

He's bound to find her.

INGER: What's it like down there?

ELISABETH: It's unbelievably beautiful here.

Pause.

I think maybe I could live here my whole life. I don't know, I think so, or thought so, before, before she disappeared, but now –

Pause.

I just want to come home.

INGER: Is it hot?

ELISABETH: Yes, it's hot, and even now, late in the evening, it's tempting to go for a swim.

Pause.

There's no one swimming though.

INGER: No?

ELISABETH: Everyone's looking for your sister. I can see it from my window, the streets are empty but up in the mountains there are tiny, tiny lights from people going round looking for her although it's completely dark out.

Pause.

Hundreds of people walking through the woods with lanterns looking for Rakel.

Pause.

I'm just going to have a bite to eat, then I'm going out to search with all the others.

Pause.

I've never been involved in anything like it. Something more beautiful.

Pause.

It's like she's brought people together in a way none of us have –

Pause.

Inger, are you there?

Pause.

You understand what I mean?

INGER: I –

Pause.

think so.

ELISABETH: Now I'm thinking, that this –

Pause.

This is the biggest thing I've ever experienced.

Pause.

It's like nothing in my life will ever surpass it, this summer, the feeling of doing something together with others, the sense of community.

Pause.

But, listen –

Pause.

Everyone's looking for her, more and more people, nobody's giving up, everyone wants the same thing. That we'll find Rakel.

Pause.

And we're going to find her.

INGER: You think so? You really think so?

ELISABETH: Yes.

INGER: Thank you!

ELISABETH: But now I have to go. And you should probably go to bed. I'm going to have a lightning-fast dinner.

INGER: Do they eat so late?

ELISABETH: Yeah, isn't that brilliant!

INGER: Elisabeth –

ELISABETH: Bye bye!

INGER: Be careful.

Scene 9

Enter RAKEL. She stands there bewildered. ELISABETH seems not to see her at first.

ELISABETH: We were out, eating, the whole class.

Pause.

Everyone who'd been looking all day until late at night for nearly a week –

Pause.

Because she'd been away for five days now.

Pause.

We all got up, stared at her, her father, the man from the embassy, the interpreter, the Italians we'd got to know –

Pause.

She didn't say anything, we asked and asked – what's happened? Where have you been?

RAKEL: I don't know.

ELISABETH: And her father just held around her, Rakel, he cried –

RAKEL: Don't cry. I'm here, aren't I –

ELISABETH: What have you been doing, has someone –

RAKEL: No, don't ask –

ELISABETH: Has someone hurt you?

RAKEL: No, no, I –

Pause.

I don't know.

Enter all the friends (in Norway) – EMBLA, YLVA, JACOB and ANDRÉ, and finally her little sister, INGER. They look towards ELISABETH and RAKEL, as if they are far away.

EMBLA: André! She's back, they've found her, she's come back, she's not dead –

ELISABETH: She just came walking across a field, out of nothing, out of the dark, and over to where we were sitting having dinner, down by the beach.

Pause.

I can touch her, hold her –

ELISABETH embraces RAKEL, holds around her.

YLVA: How does she look? How is she? Has –

Pause.

Anything happened to her? Or –

Pause.

Is she just the same?

Pause.

Is she herself?

The music is heard, the same music as was played at the discothèque when she disappeared, and everyone, apart from RAKEL, begins to dance; they talk while they are dancing –

ANDRÉ: Has she spoken to her dad? How's he taking it?

Pause.

What are they saying, is she injured, was she helped, by anyone who –

Pause.

Who can explain what's happened.

EMBLA: What does she say? What's she said?

ELISABETH: She's not saying anything, just that –

EMBLA: They've found her –

INGER: Thank you, God –

ELISABETH: We shouldn't be sad on her account.

YLVA: How strange.

ANDRÉ: I knew it, I knew she'd come back –

JACOB: What an unbelievable fuss, over nothing –

YLVA: What are you saying –

JACOB: Sorry –

YLVA: You only ever think about yourself –

283

JACOB: I'm sorry, but –

Pause.

Am I the only one who's angry with her?

Pause.

If all this is her own fault?

EMBLA: Are you absolutely sure it's her, one hundred per cent
sure –

ANDRÉ: that nothing bad's happened to her?

YLVA: You just clutch on to her, Elisabeth.

Pause.

Don't let her go. Don't let her be on her own. It's you
that'll have to look after her, until she comes home.

Pause.

And tell her.

Pause.

That we're here.

Pause.

And that we're waiting for her.

Pause.

And that we still love her.

ELISABETH embraces RAKEL, holds her tight.

Scene 10

INGER and ANDRÉ are sitting together. They keep glancing up, towards the sky.

ANDRÉ: Are you excited?

INGER: Yes. It's strange to think about it.

Pause.

That she's up there. I often think about it.

Pause.

That we can fly. It's stranger than we think. That we can be up in the air.

Pause.

Now she's on her way home, through the clouds. They'll be landing soon and then they'll be coming here.

Pause.

Her and Elisabeth. And Dad.

Pause.

Poor him. He doesn't know what to do or what to say.

ANDRÉ: Have you spoken to her? Since she came back?

INGER: I didn't know what to say, I couldn't say a word.

Pause.

It's all too much for me.

Pause.

I didn't manage to say anything apart from –

Pause.

Rakel?

Pause.

And –

ANDRÉ: And she, what did she say, just hearing your voice, must have been –

INGER: Weird, can hardly understand it, she just said that –

Pause.

There's nothing to be afraid of anymore.

Pause.

What's happened to her? What's she done? Why doesn't she say anything about what's happened?

Pause.

Dad says that she refuses to talk about it.

Is she ill?

ANDRÉ: Only Rakel knows that.

INGER: But she won't say anything!

ANDRÉ: Won't she?

INGER: No.

Pause.

She doesn't want to talk to anybody, I don't understand it.

ANDRÉ: Not Elisabeth –

INGER: Not even. She's in despair.

Pause.

Rakel won't even talk to Dad or tell him anything. Not a word.

Pause.

But I'm so looking forward to seeing her.

ANDRÉ: Me too.

INGER: I hope she's still my sister.

EMBLA comes across to them.

EMBLA: I think she's wondering a bit where you are. Not that she's looking for you, but –

INGER: Who?

EMBLA: Your mum.

INGER: Did she say so?

EMBLA: I think you'd better get off home anyway.

Pause.

Go on then!

INGER hurries off home.

ANDRÉ: Are they worried about her?

EMBLA: I don't know.

ANDRÉ: But you just said –

EMBLA: Oh, that was just a little white lie –

Pause.

I haven't seen her mum, I just wanted to be alone with you, for once.

ANDRÉ: That was naughty.

EMBLA: I know. But –

Pause.

Rakel'll be back this evening or tomorrow morning perhaps.

Pause.

We're going to have to talk to her, tell her –

Pause.

It's an awful thing to say, but I've dreamed and hoped, without wanting to, that she'd never come back.

Pause.

What sort of person am I?

ANDRÉ: That's how you think without actually wanting it.

EMBLA: But, what about us, now? How can we tell the truth? That you chatted me up, or I chatted you up, while she was maybe being killed or tortured or, ahhhh –

Pause.

We didn't know what had happened, did we, it could have been so much worse, even if she's home now, and –

Pause.

You could have said something.

ANDRÉ: What should I have said, I don't even know what I –

EMBLA: You're still in love with her.

Pause.

You just used me.

Pause.

Now she's back, you can just chuck me away again.

EMBLA runs off. ANDRÉ is left standing alone. Then he leaves too, in the opposite direction.

Scene 11

All the friends, except ANDRÉ, collect outside the school.

JACOB: Hi, how's it going?

EMBLA: Have you seen Rakel?

ELISABETH: She's talking with someone, a psychologist, I think, or the police. She wanted to go on her own. Her parents weren't allowed. She refused.

YLVA: So where are they? Her parents?

ELISABETH: They're at home.

JACOB: Ok. I see.

Pause.

We're supposed to just wait here, without knowing that she's coming.

YLVA: But, will she want to see us?

ELISABETH: I don't know. She rang and said she was with the police. To help with enquiries. And to talk with the psychologist.

JACOB: Of course she wants to see us, that's why she said she was here.

ELISABETH: She hasn't said anything otherwise.

EMBLA: There's something I've been wondering about.

Pause.

How did you know she was gone? Was it you who reported it? To the police?

Pause.

It must have been dreadful.

ELISABETH: Yes.

Pause.

I reported it, but not until the day after. I couldn't report her just because she was out late.

Pause.

Even if I was anxious the whole evening.

EMBLA: Like you knew. Like you knew something horrible was going to happen.

ELISABETH: I don't exactly know where I was, we were all out drinking, the whole language class, it was the last evening, wasn't it, and I really began to be able to speak Italian, so I just talked to everyone I met, I love Italian, I love speaking Italian. We were at a disco and I was dancing –

Pause.

The day afterwards I woke up and was stressed about having enough time to pack. And when I was finally done, I knocked on her door. But nobody opened. So

I went down, into the canteen, but nobody had seen her, so I ran out, to the cafe we usually went to, round in the streets, I shouted her name and must've been totally mad, then –

Pause.

And then there were more who started looking for her,
it got dark, and I wasn't allowed to come home, I had to
stay, and had to talk to the police, and I understood, we all
understood, that something awful had happened.

Pause.

It's the strangest thing I've ever experienced, it's nearly
so strange that I don't know how I'm supposed to go on
living, and I know it sounds horrible –

Pause.

Now that she's back.

Pause.

At the same time it's fantastic.

Pause.

Imagine, wherever I went in Pietrasanta, people
recognised me, they knew I was called Elisabeth, that
I was from Norway and had lost my best friend.

Pause.

They came over to me and held me and hugged me and
cried, "it'll be alright", they said, "she'll come back",
"don't be scared", they said, and –

Pause.

Then they held me till I stopped –

YLVA: Don't cry!

ELISABETH: I'm still looking for her, even if I know
she's back.

YLVA: Rakel!

EMBLA: There she is.

RAKEL: Where's André?

>*(To EMBLA)* Isn't he here?

EMBLA: Have you spoken to him?

RAKEL: No.

EMBLA: Strange.

EMBLA: Can't you tell us –

RAKEL: What?

EMBLA: What happened, how you are, about, tell us about
>Italy – I don't know, I just want to hear that you're alright.

RAKEL: I miss Pietrasanta already.

>*Pause.*

>What I liked about Italy, at least Pietrasanta, was how they
>were so different from us.

>*Pause.*

>They were concerned about different things, the ones
>I met anyway.

>*Pause.*

>They notice the financial crisis in a totally different
>way from us, the difference between north and south
>is enormous, the class differences, you've no idea, the
>gender roles, Catholicism –

>*Pause.*

>Everything, absolutely everything. But they wanted to do
>something, with their lives, with reality – *(pause)* – that's
>what I liked about them.

Pause.

They were in the middle of a crisis, they had no money, almost all of them, but they didn't care about it.

Pause.

It wasn't important.

Pause.

They didn't care about money.

(Looks at ELISABETH.) Those I met anyway.

Pause.

There was something wholly true about them, something honest. Unlike –

RAKEL looks at ELISABETH, at JACOB.

RAKEL: Haven't you told him –

ELISABETH: What?

Enter ANDRÉ, who stands a little aside at first.

RAKEL: Elisabeth got together with a boy down there. She had a boyfriend, nearly from the first day. I have to say it, Jacob, it's true. I'm not willing to lie anymore. Not for myself, or for anyone else. Sorry.

JACOB: I – don't believe you.

Pause.

Why hasn't she said anything herself?

Pause.

Elisabeth? Is it –

RAKEL: I'm just saying what I know. What's true.
(Looks at ANDRÉ.) André – *(pause)* – how are you?

ANDRÉ: I don't know. I don't know anything, until –

Pause.

You tell me what happened, how you really are, you must tell me.

Pause.

If you haven't –

(Looks at the others.) If she hasn't just said?

RAKEL: There's nothing to tell.

Pause.

I don't remember anything.

Pause.

And I don't want to remember either.

ELISABETH: I can't be dealing with this.

RAKEL: The last thing I remember is only that I left the disco because I hated being there, I hated myself for being there, I wanted to get away. Outside it was as if something was pulling me even further away.

Pause.

This is not my world, I thought, and I remember waving at an old woman who was standing in her kitchen,

washing herself in the kitchen sink, there was a crucifix on the wall, I waved to her and couldn't hear the music from the disco anymore, I couldn't hear the cars or anything, it felt as if I was floating and I was being drawn away, further and further.

Pause.

And then everything's black.

Pause.

The memories are gone, they're just shadows,
I can't see them, but they can see me, everything –

Pause.

Until I saw Elisabeth and the others again.

Pause.

On the beach.

(Looks at the others.) Sitting and eating.

Pause.

I saw my father too.

Pause.

And now I can see you.

The friends look at RAKEL, gradually coming closer.

YLVA: What was it like, coming back?

RAKEL: I don't know. I don't think I've understood it
completely yet, the depth of it.

Pause.

What do you think, Elisabeth?

Pause.

How was I?

ELISABETH: I really don't know. How could I know?

RAKEL: Ylva!

Pause.

What is it?

Pause.

You're looking at me like –

YLVA: I'm so happy you're back. You're so nice, look happy, and you're a bit strange, but you're lovely, you're lovely in that dress. You're yourself, but totally different, yourself and someone else at the same time.

RAKEL: Would you like it? My dress, you can have it, I don't need it.

Pause.

Say yes, I don't need it anymore, it's yours.

Pause.

I've got a bikini underneath –

YLVA: No, no, that's not what I meant –

YLVA stops her, so that she does not take off her dress. It becomes almost like an embrace.

ELISABETH: She gave away everything before she disappeared.

Pause.

She didn't need anything, she said, just gave it away, her clothes, books, she didn't need anything, she didn't want anything, and –

Pause.

And it's not true, Jacob, what she said.

Pause.

She doesn't remember anything, she said so herself.

Pause.

How could she know what I was doing when she doesn't even know what she was doing herself?

Pause.

Jacob – you have to believe me.

JACOB: Is it true, Rakel?

RAKEL: I have to go home.

Pause.

My parents are waiting for me.

Pause.

I don't think they've quite understood that I'm back.

Pause.

See you –

YLVA: Rakel!

Pause.

You've no idea, I'm so infinitely happy, that you're back.

Scene 12

ANDRÉ stands alone. RAKEL goes over to him.

RAKEL: There you are.

ANDRÉ: Yes.

Pause.

Look, that letter you sent me –

RAKEL: Yes? Shouldn't I have sent it?

ANDRÉ: Yes, no, I don't know, but –

Pause.

You broke up just before you left, and then you write a letter where it seems like you –

Pause.

Couldn't stand living like the person you are. Or were. It sounded like –

Pause.

Like you hated yourself and the whole world. It was painful to read it.

Pause.

Do you see?

Pause.

As if the world was a better place without you?

Pause.

Hi –

Enter EMBLA.

RAKEL: Embla, nice.

ANDRÉ: I want you to take your letter back.

Pause.

Maybe you'll understand more from reading it.

Pause.

Anyway, it just makes me sad.

ANDRÉ gives her the letter.

RAKEL takes it, puts it in her back pocket. She looks for a long time at EMBLA, and then at ANDRÉ.

RAKEL: So nice that you've found each other.

ANDRÉ: What are you talking about?

EMBLA: We're not –

RAKEL: I can see it.

Pause.

It's not something I'm making up.

Pause.

But, it's nice.

Pause.

The best thing that could happen, now that I'm here.

Pause.

I used to think that I had to disappear for others to be happy, but it's fantastic, it's perfect –

Pause.

To see that you can find each other, and that I can be here and see that.

Pause.

I can't understand why I said what I said about Elisabeth, I just want her to be happy, after all.

Pause.

But it's said now.

EMBLA: You're crazy, we've never been together, I would never –

RAKEL: It's ok, it's nice, it –

RAKEL reaches out to her, tries to embrace her, but EMBLA walks away.

ANDRÉ: She's got a bad conscience.

RAKEL: She doesn't need to.

ANDRÉ: And you?

Pause.

Did you have an Italian boyfriend down there?

RAKEL: No.

Pause.

That's the last thing I was thinking about.

Pause.

When I broke off with you, it was because I didn't want to have a boyfriend.

Pause.

It wasn't *you* there was anything wrong with.

Pause.

You're perfect. It's me –

Pause.

There's something wrong with, if there's anything wrong with anyone.

ANDRÉ: Is it true that you've been talking to a psychologist?

RAKEL: Yes.

Pause.

The doctors and psychologists say that I've had a psychosis. That I've actually been ill and that I'm healthy now. And that's right in a way. At least better.

ANDRÉ: But how?

Pause.

If no one at all has noticed?

Pause.

You don't go round being ill without you or anyone else having the faintest idea about it.

RAKEL: I know, it's weird.

Pause.

But I also know, that I've gone round hiding, how sad I've been, for the whole of the last year.

Pause.

So I've hidden it. The grief.

Pause.

For absolutely everyone I have loved.

ANDRÉ: In the letter you talked about –

RAKEL: I thought I wanted to die. No –

Pause.

I don't want to say anything else, it's impossible to talk about it.

Pause.

Even with you.

Pause.

I'm so upset, André, I just want to be alone. Even if that's the last thing I want.

Exit RAKEL, ANDRÉ remains standing.

Waits.

Enter EMBLA. They embrace each other.

Scene 13

Enter ELISABETH, walking. She stops, throws a pebble against a window.

ELISABETH: Rakel.

Pause.

Rakel!

Pause.

Rakel – I need to talk to you, can't you –

RAKEL: Ok, I'm coming. I'll come out.

Pause.

I must just tell my parents, so they won't be scared. They're sitting watching TV.

RAKEL comes out.

RAKEL: Hi.

ELISABETH: I hope I didn't –

RAKEL: No. You didn't wake me.

Pause.

Not that it had mattered anyway.

Pause.

Is it anything in particular?

ELISABETH: Why didn't you tell me?

Pause.

We've known each other all our lives, we were together every single day for four weeks, we *(pause)* talked about everything, and then you haven't told me –

RAKEL: What?

ELISABETH: Why didn't you tell me, that you'd broken up?

Pause.

I thought we shared everything?

Pause.

And then the truth turns out that I don't know anything about you. It's horrible to think about it.

Pause.

Ever since I was little, I thought –

Pause.

We were best friends and always would be.

Pause.

And that you and André, well, I don't know.

Pause.

And then you break up, without a word.

Pause.

And give away my secrets –

RAKEL: I know that it sounds weird, but –

Pause.

I was already somewhere else. I didn't think –

Pause.

About telling it to anyone, to you or anyone else.

ELISABETH: I walked for hours on end in the woods, along the ridge, up and down steep hillsides just looking for you.

Pause.

I cried myself to sleep every night.

Pause.

And thought it was my fault, that you were gone.

Pause.

I was so angry with you. And angry with myself.

Pause.

What had I said or done, I thought,

Pause.

Should I have looked after you a bit better, thought less about myself, I –

RAKEL: I understand. Poor you.

ELISABETH: And, why did you say, that I'd been with other guys?

Pause.

Nobody needed to know that.

Pause.

Least of all Jacob.

RAKEL: Because it's true. You know it is. I saw you. I heard
you. We had rooms next to each other. It was –

Pause.

I don't know, I'm not going to say any more,
I regret it, but.

Pause.

I felt sorry for Jacob.

ELISABETH: It's worse for him now. He's inconsolable.

Pause.

He threatened to –

RAKEL: But it's not my fault. You have to talk to him. You
must tell him everything.

ELISABETH: I searched for you, hour after hour for a whole
week, in that terrible heat.

RAKEL: And I'm so grateful. That you wanted to help me.

Pause.

Or my parents. And Inger, my little sister, poor her –

Pause.

But, I can't –

Pause.

I can't say something that isn't true. It is true –

Pause.

That you got together with unbelievably many guys down there?

ELISABETH: I was so happy when I saw you, and realised, that it was you, that you were yourself, now

Pause.

I don't know if I can bear to see you again.

Pause.

Now it's you that's lost me.

Exit ELISABETH. RAKEL is left standing alone outside the house.

INGER comes out. It seems like she's been crying. She is in her nightclothes.

RAKEL: What's the matter?

Pause.

Inger?

INGER: I don't know. Everything is –

Pause.

Strange. Everybody –

Pause.

Is crying. Mum and Dad in their bedroom, Elisabeth here –

RAKEL: She's not crying –

INGER: She tried to hide it, but I saw –

Pause.

She was crying, from the bedroom. And I cry when I go to bed and go to sleep.

RAKEL: It's difficult. Perhaps it was –

Pause.

Better, somehow, when I was missing?

Pause.

Or did they argue, like they usually do?

INGER: No, we were just sad.

RAKEL: But –

Pause.

You can't be sad now, now that I've come home, can you?

INGER: Yes – and it's that

Pause.

That's so strange.

RAKEL: I know.

Pause.

I'm sad too.

Pause.

Even if I'm happy.

Pause.

At least, I'm glad to see you.

INGER: Hear that?

Pause.

They're calling for you, they've just been in your room looking for you, I guess they'll hear us talking and calm down.

Pause.

I'm your little sister, but it's you they're calling.

Pause.

It's strange.

Pause.

When you're thirteen, nearly fourteen... fourteen, that is if anyone remembers I have a birthday –

Pause.

I'm sure they're going to forget it now, it's strange, being surrounded by the feeling of having disappeared for good.

Pause.

I was here just for a moment, for a few short days, when you were missing.

Pause.

And now I've disappeared again.

RAKEL: Inger –

INGER goes into the house. RAKEL remains outside.

Scene 14

Someone stands alone on the beach.

ITALIAN BOY: Now the summer will soon be over.

Pause.

Everyone from the language school has travelled home, all the girls, their names and faces fade into each other, become one person, one face, tight shorts and a T-shirt where something almost illegible is written, you could read it a thousand times.

Pause.

Sometimes we talk about it. How pale their skin was when they came, how quickly they got tanned, never sunburnt, they made sure of that, it's like there was one single girl we all fell in love with, one single girl we were with, one single face, one single kiss that didn't belong to anyone.

Pause.

Apart from Rakel. We never talk about her, but we think about her all the time, we might be sitting on the beach, swimming, playing football or at a party, all of us, then one of us says –

Pause.

Do you remember Rakel, the girl who disappeared, I wonder what –

Pause.

And then everything goes completely silent between us, and we try to see her, as she was.

Scene 15

YLVA, ELISABETH, JACOB, EMBLA, then ANDRÉ, and finally all the friends enter.

YLVA: What you up to?

ELISABETH: Nothing special.

YLVA: You two together again?

ELISABETH: Yes.

JACOB: Yes.

YLVA: Good.

Pause.

Has anyone seen anything of Rakel?

ELISABETH: No. Not for a while.

INGER: Hi –

ELISABETH: Hi –

YLVA: Inger, good to see you. How's your sister?

INGER: I don't know, perhaps I'm too young to understand how she is. Why don't you ask her?

YLVA: I never see her.

JACOB: Has she locked herself in or what?

INGER: There she is.

ELISAETH: Rakel –

YLVA: So nice to see you!

Pause.

I almost didn't dare visit you, I was afraid –

Pause.

that you didn't want any visitors.

RAKEL: I'm sure I needed to be on my own for a while, at least that's what everyone –

Pause.

I've spoken to says.

YLVA: I think I must've walked past your house a thousand times, tiptoed through the garden, almost rung the bell, but –

Pause.

It must be difficult coming home. Here. After such –

Pause.

An experience.

JACOB: Or you needed just a bit more time, to make up more to say –

ELISABETH: Jacob!

JACOB: about what happened to you.

YLVA: What an idiot you are, Jacob.

Pause.

Come on, sit yourself down, Rakel. Tell us.

Pause.

Don't you remember anything, anything else?

Pause.

Or is it too painful to think about it?

RAKEL: You lot don't believe me, do you? You think I remember everything, but that I don't want to say anything, you –

ELISABETH: That's it.

Pause.

It's true. I don't believe you anymore.

EMBLA: I don't understand, that when you think back, then –

JACOB: She remembers what she wants to remember –

EMBLA: What is it that you do remember?

RAKEL: I remember the last thing I saw.

Pause.

I walked out of the town, through a park, by some fields, and up onto the ridge, which I kind of followed or didn't really have any other choice, all the time it was getting darker –

INGER: Weren't you scared?

RAKEL: No, I wasn't scared, not scared of anybody or anything.

Pause.

Everything was lovely, warm and beautiful, and the sound of the sea got louder the further away from the sea I went. It got cool, or cooler, it smelled of flowers.

YLVA: Isn't it strange, or scary, not to know exactly where you've been or what's happened to you?

RAKEL: The scariest thing was coming back.

Pause.

When I saw the people searching, I got scared. The woods were full of people in dark clothing walking in ranks, like soldiers, staring at the ground.

Pause.

I didn't even understand that the people I saw down there, in the valley below me, were people searching. And that it was me they were looking for.

Pause.

I saw my father in the wood, and I didn't understand, what was he doing in the wood, in Italy, he couldn't be two places at once, I thought, he was back home in Norway, wasn't he?

Pause.

Not here, in Pietrasanta.

Pause.

So I ran away, and then I was gone again. I could've come back a number of times, now I don't understand why I didn't.

Pause.

What was I scared of?

INGER: You saw him? That's weird, if you saw dad, and didn't realise it was him, then you must've been –

RAKEL: Yes,, but I didn't want to understand that I was missing.

Pause.

I walked around in the woods, in the mountains, in the empty villages, I remember a church, where the roof was gone, and it could rain straight in, I slept there, and I walked around, hour after hour, without understanding where I was, day after day.

JACOB: Empty villages? That sounds a bit odd.

ELISABETH: But it's true.

Pause.

There are lots of abandoned villages, with absolutely no people, empty houses, no one wants to live there anymore, they're ghost towns. Sometimes teenagers go there to get drunk and to –

JACOB: It's like she's making it all up.

ELISABETH: Jacob –

JACOB: We've talked about it.

Pause.

Haven't we talked about it, Elisabeth?

Pause.

Every time we see you, there's something new, or something else, first you don't remember anything, then you were ill or depressed –

Pause.

Or what was it, psychotic, was that what you called it?

Pause.

Teenage psychosis?

Pause.

So, what else was there, I get in a muddle myself, what else was there –

Pause.

You wanted to kill yourself.

INGER: Teenage psychosis –

Pause.

What's that?

RAKEL: It's true, it's not a lie.

Pause.

I was ill, and it doesn't help that no one believes me.

ELISABETH: I think you're perfectly well, you are now at least, and you ran off to make yourself more interesting. To be perfectly honest.

RAKEL: But Jacob's right.

Pause.

The truth is I don't dare say anything, because I know, that you –

Pause.

Won't believe me.

YLVA: You could have tried talking to us.

EMBLA: Been honest. Not just –

Pause.

Criticising others.

Enter ANDRÉ. Only RAKEL sees him. She nods to him cautiously, he nods back.

ELISABETH: I'm sure you just wanted to run away. But you didn't dare. There's no more to it than that. No psychosis, no breakdown, no nothing.

Pause.

You're just spineless.

Pause.

You liked the idea of us missing you, maybe you were at a hotel, or home with some boy you'd got to know.

Pause.

It wouldn't surprise me.

Pause.

If it was all lies.

YLVA: Elisabeth, you don't know everything either, you've even said –

Pause.

That you were totally gone too, that you were a different person down there, someone you didn't know, but always –

Pause.

Wanted to be, you didn't know what you were doing, you said –

ELISABETH: But you don't need, Rakel –

ANDRÉ: I believe you, Rakel. Whatever you say. Or however difficult it is to find the words to describe –

YLVA: We want to believe you, all of us –

RAKEL: I remember waving goodbye,

Pause.

And –

ANDRÉ: Just tell them what you told me –

EMBLA: Have you been talking to her?

Pause.

Why haven't you said anything?

ANDRÉ: You walked for many hours, the whole night.

Pause.

You saw a –

Pause.

What was it you called it,

Pause.

A heavenly being, and –

EMBLA: *(In disbelief.)* The Virgin Mary or something like that?

ANDRÉ: A saint, perhaps?

RAKEL: It was a saint, or a kind of angel, yes –

Pause.

a heavenly being, and...

Pause.

I don't know if it was a man or a woman, I'm not sure. It's not that simple.

Pause.

Then, she, or he, spoke to me.

Pause.

Yes, I can describe her. She, or he, was almost naked. Her whole body was covered with wounds but it didn't look like they hurt her, or him. She pulled out an arrow, a kind of old-fashioned arrow, like from a bow and arrow, out of her body.

Pause.

Yes.

Pause.

I understood, that I had the ability to soothe his pain.

EMBLA: Was *that* what the angel said?

YLVA: Let her talk –

INGER: I don't understand what you're talking about, can't you just –

INGER leaves.

YLVA: Inger, don't –

RAKEL: Let her go. Poor thing. I shouldn't have said –

ELISABETH: I don't believe any of this, I really don't.

Pause.

I can't be dealing with this anymore. I –

Pause.

Searched for you, for days, I've tried to comfort you, and forgive you, and I know you've had a tough time, but come on –

Pause.

No, I can't be dealing with this,

Pause.

I just want to go.

RAKEL: Here –

RAKEL takes out the letter from her back pocket, the one she got back from ANDRÉ.

RAKEL: Elisabeth –

Pause.

Won't you read this?

Pause.

It's all there –

ELISABETH takes the letter, looks at it, then throws it to the ground. And leaves. JACOB watches her. Then he picks up the letter. And hands it back to RAKEL.

RAKEL: Yes, please, go –

Pause.

I need to be alone.

(Takes the letter.) Thanks.

JACOB: Rakel, I –

Then he hurries away. ANDRÉ and YLVA remain behind.

ANDRÉ: I believe you, Rakel –

RAKEL: I touched him. Or her. I knew, that if I could pull out one of those arrows, I'd make it easier for him.

Pause.

Or her.

Pause.

And I understood that by pulling out one of these arrows I'd show –

Pause.

That I'd understood why he, or she, had come –

Pause.

She wanted to show me that I could make the world a better place. That I could soothe people's pain, not just here, but –

Pause.

She didn't say how.

Pause.

What I'm going to do now, I don't know. I remember thinking, if I could only take one of those arrows with me, that I'd have proof, then you'd believe me –

YLVA: I believe you –

RAKEL: But the light was so bright, and –

Pause.

I was so weak,

Pause.

I got weaker and weaker, and –

Pause.

Even before she disappeared, I hoped –

Pause.

I would see her again.

YLVA reaches out to her, just about touches her arm, and, at the same moment, RAKEL faints and collapses to the ground.

Scene 16

RAKEL is alone. It may appear that some time has passed. While she speaks, it happens that she looks straight up into the air.

RAKEL: Yes, of course.

Pause.

I understand it's difficult for them.

Pause.

Yes, it must feel like that. They have lost me once, so –

Pause.

No. It's impossible to explain.

Pause.

That's why I didn't want to say anything. And that's why it looked like I was lying about everything.

Pause.

Sorry?

Pause.

No, no, I couldn't say that. Not worse either. But that could be the medicines.

Pause.

Yes, yes, I have a better relationship with them now. There's a lot we can't talk about and I still think they're better off without me.

Pause.

There's nothing I want. Or anything I've asked for.

Pause.

If I get well?

Pause.

The only thing I know is –

Pause.

I'm not young anymore.

Pause.

Are we done now?